Moments pass as I listen to our quickened breathing. We are unmoving, awkward together, and I know this moment is as much a shock to her as it is to me.

But as our breathing settles, I begin to feel her fingertips roll along my spine. I bury my face in the nape of her neck and breathe deeply, remembering her scent, memorizing the feel of her smooth skin against my cheek.

Joanna comes to mind, and I push the thought of her aside. Forcefully. Purposely. There will be plenty of time to think about Joanna later, I know. At this moment all I know, all I care about, is that I am holding Grace Sullivan in my arms.

Just Yesterday

BY
LINDA HILL

THE NAIAD PRESS, INC.
1998

Printed in the United States of America on acid-free paper
First Edition

Editor: Lila Empson
Cover designer: Bonnie Liss (Phoenix Graphics)
Typesetter: Sandi Stancil

Library of Congress Cataloging-in-Publication Data

Hill, Linda, 1958 –
    Just yesterday / by Linda Hill.
        p.   cm.
    ISBN 1-56280-219-4   (alk. paper)
    1. Lesbians – Fiction   I. Title.
PS3558.I392J87   1998
813'.54—dc21   98-13222
                                                                      CIP

For Mary

Acknowledgments

Thanks to Barb, Deb, and the others who weighed in with an opinion on how this story should end when I agonized over the final chapters. In the end it was my editor, Lila Empson, who made the final choice. I thank her for deciding which ending "rang true."

Special thanks to Kathy, the constant in my life. And to Cheryl, who always understood without question or reproach. *And believed.*

About the Author

Originally from the Midwest, Linda Hill now makes her home in the Boston area. Her previous novels include *Never Say Never,* and *Class Reunion.* Her fourth novel, *Change of Heart,* will be published by Naiad in 1999.

Chapter 1

Joanna and I stand just inside the doorway, our noses pressed against the windowpane. As the last car pulls out of the driveway and starts down the street, I lean back against the door and wipe my brow, feigning relief.

"Whew. I thought they'd never leave."

Joanna pushes my shoulder playfully. "Don't say that. It was sweet of everyone to come over tonight." She turns and walks back through the hallway and into the kitchen, continuing to reprimand me sweetly. "It was *our* anniversary, after all."

Within moments, she begins running water in the sink, stacking dishes, and pouring detergent into the mix.

"I know. It was very nice. But it's after midnight." It is incomprehensible to me that she is doing the dishes. At midnight. On our ten-year anniversary. Frankly, I have other ideas in mind for how we should be spending the next hour. But I don't want to make a big deal about it. Nonchalance is what I'm going for. After all, it has been so long since we've made love that I'm not even very comfortable suggesting the idea.

The dishrag is in one hand and a plate in the other as she begins to scrub in earnest. "It was nice to see everyone again," she says above the splashing of the water. "Do you think we were dishonest? Maybe we should have told them about us."

"It would have been inappropriate to announce at our anniversary party that we've decided to split up." I can't help the sarcasm that creeps into my voice. The truth is that I don't really want to split up, that I am hoping that maybe tonight we can start over. "Besides," I try for humor. "I thought we agreed on a separation. Not a divorce."

Her smile is discerning, and I feel my anxiety growing.

"Honey, let's leave the dishes for now. We can do them in the morning." She throws me a look that says she knows that while I've said the word *we*, I really mean *she*. We have, after all, been together for ten years. I'm not fooling her for a minute.

I grin a bit sheepishly and move to stand behind her. My arms find their way around her waist, and I press my lips to her neckline. "Why don't we just go

2

upstairs to bed?" I ask. "I was hoping maybe we could make love."

I can feel her spine stiffening. "Liz, we agreed."

I try to fight my disappointment while mentally kicking myself. My heart just isn't into the separation idea, but I know better than to set myself up like this. "Joanna —"

"Maybe it's time for one of us to think about moving out."

"Move out?" It feels as though she's kicked me in the stomach. I'm not even used to the idea that we're splitting up, and she's already got my bags packed. The look on my face must screech volumes because she is instantly contrite.

"Honey, I'm sorry. That was a stupid thing to say. I'm just exhausted." Is it my imagination, or is she scrubbing a plate that she has already washed and set aside to dry?

"It's okay," I lie. A slew of things come to my mind. Questions I want to ask. Statements I want to make. Anger and sarcasm struggle in my brain. But neither wins. I keep my lips carefully sealed and give the woman I love a quick squeeze before releasing her. "I'm going down to the darkroom to putter around. I'll be up soon, okay?"

She nods and smiles. "Okay. Good night, honey. Happy anniversary."

"Happy anniversary." I manage a smile before slipping through the door that leads down to the basement and my makeshift office. My hand finds each light switch automatically as I make my way past the laundry room and into the safety of my darkroom.

I flip on the light and glance around, eyes not

focusing on anything. My body finds its familiar position on the stool that sits before a huge photo enlarger. A deep sigh racks my lungs as my fist lifts and begins to tap my forehead quietly.

"Hello?" I speak aloud to myself, something I only do in the privacy of this very room. "Hello? What's wrong with this picture?" I glance around the room, at the photographs and negatives hanging along the walls, and manage to laugh at my own pun. My eyes focus on a photograph of an elderly man sitting on a park bench and deftly lifting a sandwich to his lips. I direct my comments to him.

"It's my anniversary," I tell him. "Ten years." He doesn't budge. "I know. You think I should be upstairs celebrating with my wife instead of hanging around down here talking to you. You're right. I agree completely." I say the last few words grimly, as my self-imposed chill begins to thaw and the hurt and anger of the moment spills forth.

I don't know why I set myself up tonight. I don't know why I thought tonight would be different from any other night. And even though we had agreed last week that it probably made sense for us to split up, it wasn't something that I really believed would happen. My head is shaking back and forth as I bite back frustration.

I don't know what happened to us. It began with subtle rejection. Something that I never really wanted to admit was happening. So I learned to avoid it. I stopped laying my hand on her thigh in the car. Stopped curling up next to her on the couch after dinner. Stopped rolling over in bed and holding her all night. Stopped asking if she'd like to make love. I learned that lesson quickly. Three years of rejection is a mighty long time.

At least I think it's been about three years. I can't remember, exactly. I only know that it was before Sophie, our first cat, had died. We'd adopted Ginger and MaryAnn a few months later. And they were nearly three years old now. So three years seemed a good estimate, if not exact.

What happened? I have asked myself, and Joanna, that question so many times. I had believed our life was perfect for so many years. *Lesbian bed death.* The thought crosses my mind and I banish it, refusing to be a statistic.

The shrill of the ringing telephone sends my heart jumping, and I grab the receiver from its cradle. Who in the hell could be calling at this hour?

"Hello," I bark.

"Hi." One syllable from a voice from so long ago. One syllable. My heart skips a beat with recognition before her name even registers in my mind. "This is Grace Sullivan. Sorry to be calling so late, but is Elizabeth there?"

"Grace." The name passes my lips in a honeyed whoosh. "Hi. It's me."

"Hi." I don't miss her hesitation over the word. "I wasn't sure if you were still at this number."

Already my mind is whirling, thoughts and images spinning behind my eyes. I haven't heard that voice in what — five, six years at least.

"Still here," I answer, keeping a smile in my voice.

"Does that mean you've finally settled down?" Thirty seconds into the phone call, and already a dig.

Ten years, I nearly scream. *That's pretty damned settled, wouldn't you say?*

"Very settled," I manage instead, letting my own voice dip to mock her in reply. "I'm very settled, thank you. How are you?"

"Good," she replies briskly, already moving on. "Listen. I thought you should know. Connie's been in an accident. I don't know much about it other than what the newsboys have been able to dig up. But I called the hospital and it didn't sound good."

Connie. My heart freezes as images of my ex-lover replace those of Grace in my mind's eye.

"What happened? What did they tell you?"

"Apparently she and two other women were in a small plane that went down the night before last." Grace's voice is matter-of-fact. "She was the only survivor. I understand she was in surgery all day yesterday and hasn't regained consciousness yet."

"My god." My stomach is turning over. "What else do you know? Is she going to be all right?"

"I don't know anything else. Except that the plane was headed to Michigan. I assume for the Michigan Women's Music Festival. But I don't know for certain."

"Can't you get more information? Don't you have a lot of connections there?" Last I'd heard, Grace was working at a local television station in the news department.

"I told you. That's all the guys could dig up." She pauses briefly. "Besides, you know I like to keep my personal life private. I didn't want to start asking a bunch of questions about a plane carrying three dykes crashing on their way to a women's festival."

Now I'm exasperated. Connie could be dying, and

Grace is worried about being outed. "Well, have you talked to your friends? Don't they know anything?"

I can hear the impatience in Grace's voice. "Connie and I don't exactly run around in the same crowd."

Old and familiar annoyance comes over me as I battle my response. Connie is lying in a hospital bed, and Grace is being catty.

As if sensing my thoughts, her voice softens. "I don't mean that in a snotty way, Liz. We just don't have the same friends, that's all. I haven't seen Connie in years."

Probably not since you had an affair, I want to say, but bite my tongue.

"Anyway," she continues, "I don't know any more than that. But I thought you'd want to know."

"Thanks, Grace. Yes. I do want to know." Already my mind is moving forward, thinking of the phone calls I have to make. "I'll call her mom in the morning," I say, more to myself than to Grace.

"Let me know how she is, okay?"

"I will," I assure her, then grab for a pen while she rattles off her phone number. We say good-bye, and I place the phone back in its cradle while a kaleidoscope of thoughts and feelings collide inside me.

Connie. I cannot believe it. My hand reaches for the light switch as I stumble up the stairs. Joanna. I need Joanna.

Chapter 2

By ten o'clock the next morning my arrangements were made. I spoke briefly with Connie's sister, Charlene, who was able to tell me little more than what I'd already heard from Grace. When I asked if I'd be in the way if I came to the hospital to visit, Charlene was quick to assure me.

"God, no. Mom's up there now. I can't drag her away. She'd love to see you, and it would be good for her to have someone else around besides Wendy."

"Who's Wendy?" I'd asked.

"Connie's girlfriend. Did you ever meet her?"

I didn't want to admit that I hadn't even talked with Connie in four years, so I simply said no.

"She's kind of a trip, that one. But Connie loves her, and that's all that matters." We'd hung up shortly after that.

I made several more calls, shifting assignments around to make room until the end of the week. If Joanna thought it odd that I was leaving so suddenly, she didn't show it. She expressed genuine concern, and encouraged me to find out for myself just how Connie was doing.

Two hours later I was on the plane, staring out the window at the clouds below. It didn't occur to me until that moment that I hadn't even considered not going. I never even thought about why I'd felt it necessary to make this trip. I hadn't even hesitated. Scary, now that I was alone with my thoughts. I was about to dip farther into my past than I had ever thought I would again.

I tried reading the newspaper. After reading and rereading the same article four times, I gave in and closed my eyes. What irony that I was returning home to see Connie, and possibly Grace. Connie and Grace. I couldn't think of one without the other. It didn't matter that they barely knew each other. For me, the three of us were forever tangled. In my heart, and in my memories.

I met Connie when I was twenty-two years old. By then I had developed a love for photography and had begun working at a local processing lab. I hated most of the job — waiting on customers and printing their pictures in the one-hour lab. But what kept me there was that I had access to all of their equipment. I couldn't wait to close up the shop each night so that I could work on my own photographs. I spent most of my free time on weekends taking pictures with an old Minolta camera that my grandfather had given me. During the week, I would stay late at the lab developing my own pictures.

Connie had become a regular at the shop. She was a photography instructor at the local arts center while she was earning her teaching degree at night. It eventually took nearly eight years of night school to earn her the degree that others received in four.

At twenty-seven, Connie had white-blond hair that fell just to her shoulders. She was thin as a rail and had high cheekbones and white, creamy skin. Her eyes were a startling green, and she wore a pair of thick, wire-rimmed glasses that habitually slid down her nose. I fell for her almost instantly. She began helping me out in the lab at night, patiently teaching me subtle tricks about photography that seemed to make each photo take on a life of its own.

Connie taught me the difference between taking a picture and the art of photography. We'd spend hours at the lab. And when we ran out of film to develop, we'd spend hours over coffee while she told me her dreams and made no bones about what mine ought to be. She tried time after time to convince me to go to college, but I shrugged her off, cocky and arrogant, believing I'd make it even without that piece of paper.

We dated for two years before she finally got her degree. Within weeks, she had teaching offers from all over the country. So many that she couldn't make up her mind. But at the end of August, she packed everything she owned in her Ford wagon and took off for the West Coast. She didn't ask me to go with her, although I would have gone in a heartbeat. She promised she'd send for me, though. Once she was settled. Of course I wanted to believe her. But somewhere, deep down, I never trusted that she'd ever call and say the words. I'd gotten rather close to her family during that time, and it was Connie's mother and sister who kept me believing that one day that phone call might come.

And then I met Grace.

Even now, I can't think about Grace without hurting. Even today, my memories and emotions become instantly confused as I think back to the time we'd met. But I can't — won't — think of Grace just now. It is dangerous. That much I know. And this trip is about Connie, I remind myself. *Not about Grace.*

There's no such thing as a direct flight between Los Angeles and Champaign, Illinois. Naturally, I miss my connecting flight and end up arriving in Champaign well after dinner, much later than planned. I pick up a rental car and drive the round-about way to my hotel, purposely avoiding my old high school and the neighborhood that I'd grown up in. I had visited enough of my past via memories already today.

Skipping dinner, I flip on the local television news, unpack my suitcase, and flop down on the bed, exhausted. My last waking thought is one of wonder that all of the news anchors, including the weatherman, have been on that same station over fifteen years ago. I marvel sleepily, noting that they've barely aged at all.

I wake the next morning with a single-mindedness to get to the hospital as soon as possible. Without hesitating, I dial the phone number that Grace has given me and am somewhat relieved to get an answering machine. I explain that I'll be leaving the following afternoon and tell her to leave me a message if she can squeeze me into her schedule somehow during the next twenty-four hours. But I'm not counting on seeing her.

I hate hospitals, and being in Champaign's Saint John's does nothing to change my mind. The smell of disinfectant hangs in the air as I find the intensive care unit and brace myself for what I am about to see.

I never could have prepared myself for the scene before me. Tubes and machines and monitors and blood. My throat begins constricting, and I force myself to take slow, even breaths. *Jesus.* My stomach threatens to lurch as my vision blurs, the room becoming nothing more than blobs of color. White. Stainless steel gray. The brown-orange color of dried blood.

A white sheet is pulled tight over her torso, tucked under her armpits. Her right arm and leg are encased in plaster. Needles and tubes and tape sprinkle and cover every inch of her left arm. My eyes follow one tube and settle on the steady drip, drip of liquid in the bag above her head. The only sound is the steady beep that accompanies the green line that jumps on the heart monitor nearly every second.

I cannot recognize the swollen features of her face. But I know it's her by the white-blond strands of hair that lie against the pillow. My eyes try to avoid the matted dried blood that covers most of her scalp.

"Elizabeth? Is that you?" The voice that reaches me from my left is immediately followed by a shadow that enters my peripheral vision.

Vaguely, my mind registers the voice. But I am slow to turn and respond. "Mrs. Kaplan." Connie's mother is wrapping her arms around me, her small frame pressing against mine as she squeezes tightly.

When she finally releases me, she stands back and blinks up at me, the red of her eyes in sharp contrast to the pasty white of her skin. She appears so much older than I remember her. My eyes trace the deep lines that etch her cheeks and note that the skin that stretches across her bones seems almost translucent. I take a deep breath, the drastic change in her appearance unnerving me even more. Then we are both talking at once, awkwardly throwing out one line after another.

"I'm so sorry, Mrs. Kaplan."

"Thank you for coming, Elizabeth."

"I'm so sorry." I must have repeated the same line a half a dozen times.

"It was so sweet of you to come all this way."

I feel a prickling sensation along my spine and

sense rather than see another pair of eyes on me. Almost against my will, I lift my head and find myself frozen by the dark eyes that practically hold me in my place.

She sits stiffly in a chair at the foot of Connie's bed, slender arms crossed, dark skin smooth across high cheekbones. Her black hair is smoothed down and slicked back. A splash of red lipstick is the only bright color that adorns her features, as she is dressed completely in shades of brown.

My mouth grows dry as she lifts her chin, almost regally, and speaks without getting up.

"I'm Wendy," she announces simply, as if there is really nothing else of importance to say.

I nod, remembering Charlene's comments about Connie's girlfriend from earlier yesterday. Stepping farther into the room to shake her hand, I think better of it when I see her arms remain firmly crossed against her chest.

"Liz," I say finally, introducing myself.

"Elizabeth Grey?" Her tone doesn't change, and I'm not certain whether she is asking a question or making a statement. When I nod, she responds again, her voice unchanging. "I know who you are."

For several moments I wonder how it is that she has heard of me. Was it from Charlene or Connie's mother during the past twenty-four hours? Had Connie mentioned me in passing while enumerating the lovers in her past? Had I been the source of some heated argument between her and Connie?

If she senses my internal debate, she refuses to give any clues. We continue to stare until I can take it no longer, and I refocus on Connie's mother.

"How is she doing?" I ask stupidly. It doesn't take a surgeon to see that Connie's condition is critical.

Mrs. Kaplan's only reply is in the tight, thin line of her lips and the eyes that begin to fill. Her eyes shift to her daughter, and I follow their gaze.

I am much closer to the bed now and have to breathe deeply to steady myself. I still can't recognize my ex-lover.

My eyes catch the glint of stainless steel around her head and I squint, a sick curiosity getting the best of me as my mind begins to comprehend what I am seeing. A large, square patch of skin is exposed on the top of Connie's head where it has obviously been shaved. What appear to be two metal screws are implanted in her skull. Secured to the metal screws is a kind of braided wire, which is threaded through some sort of contraption behind Connie's head. I follow the wire and feel my stomach drop as I realize that it is attached to two large weights that hang just behind and below the head of the bed.

"She broke her neck." Her mother's voice is weak. The flash of pain that racks my insides is so complete that I cannot identify what hurts the most. My head is exploding, my heart aching, my stomach dropping. I wasn't prepared for any of this.

"You know the rules, Mrs. Kaplan," a voice booms behind me and I jump, turning to see the stern face beneath a nurse's cap eyeing each of us separately. "Only two visitors at a time. Family only."

"This is Connie's sister, Elizabeth." Mrs. Kaplan lifts her chin defiantly.

"Uh-huh." The nurse's tone makes it clear that she doesn't believe a word of it. "Just like she's her sister, too." She nods in Wendy's direction and I almost smile. Wendy is clearly as dark African American as Connie is pale-white Caucasian.

Connie's sister, Charlene, appears from behind the nurse and reaches me in two short steps, wrapping her arms around me in a quick hug. She is a younger, shorter image of Connie. Her long blond hair isn't as fine or light as Connie's, but Charlene is far more attractive in the traditional sense.

"That's it." The nurse draws herself up indignantly. "Two of you. Out. Now."

We all look at each other until I catch the pleading in Charlene's blue eyes and I remember our conversation from the day before.

"Come on, Mom." I tuck my arm under Mrs. Kaplan's elbow and try what I hope is my most charming smile. "Let's go get a cup of coffee and catch up."

She hesitates, and I give her a small nudge. "You won't be gone long, I promise. I want to spend some time with Charlene while I'm here, too."

Her eyes move from Charlene to the closed eyes of her other daughter as she lies on the bed. She is so fragile. So indecisive.

"It's okay, Mom," Charlene says softly. "Go with Liz. Connie will be okay while you're gone."

I watch the emotions flicker across the older woman's face and feel my heart constrict again. The fear on her face is plain. She is afraid that Connie will die and that she won't be there when it happens.

She stares up at me and I flash a reassuring smile. I'm rewarded with a curt nod, and then we are ushering each other from the room.

* * * * *

I remain at the hospital for most of the day, alternately walking the hallways with Charlene and her mother, then standing motionless at Connie's bedside. As the day progresses, I am able to look at her for longer periods of time.

She remains unrecognizable to me. Everything except the blond hair and the left hand that lies at her side. My eyes trace each finger and I am grateful for the familiar blunt fingertips that somehow validate my being there in a room of near strangers.

It is those fingers that I recognize. How many times had I lovingly watched those fingers hover over a photograph as it came to life on paper? Connie had swished the chemicals around in the tray, eyeing the image until it reached perfection. Then those fingers would dip down and sweep up the print, only to submerge it quickly in yet another solution.

Silently, I stand over Connie. Apologizing for all those things unsaid. For all of the mistakes we have made. Foolishly, I will her eyes to open, frustration rising as she resolutely lies still. The fear of her death is suddenly very real to me, our mortality something I'd rarely given thought to before this morning.

Just before I leave to return to my hotel, I speak to her silently. I say good-bye, even while I don't want to believe that's what I'm doing. But I know, somehow, that I might never see the startling green of her eyes again. It doesn't matter that we haven't spoken in four years. I'd always had the option to see her, to talk with her. But with death were no such options.

I return to my hotel in an emotional stupor. Part of me wants to curl up on the bed and pretend that none of it has happened. Part of me begins to obsess about Connie, and I begin replaying in my mind many of the moments we have shared. I find myself trying to remember why we broke up, but cannot.

My mind drifts to Joanna, and panic seizes me. What would I ever do if this happened to Joanna? She is my entire life.

Suddenly I miss her. Badly. Not just the woman that I'd left back in Los Angeles. I miss the way we used to be. The closeness we used to share. Five years ago I would never have made this trip alone. Yesterday she'd barely blinked when I left for the airport.

I resolve to do whatever it takes to find that closeness again. We have to find a way to make things work.

Without another thought, I reach for the phone and dial our number.

Chapter 3

Eight hours of sleep did nothing to lighten my mood. Joanna had been sympathetic but distant on the phone the night before. When I told her that I thought maybe we had made a mistake, that maybe we should give it another try, she sidestepped my concerns.

"Honey, we've talked about this for two years. You're just emotional because of Connie."

"I know I'm emotional. That's the point. Maybe I'm just realizing what's important in life." I hated feeling rebuffed. I also hated that I felt so weak and vulnerable. Especially when I knew she was probably right.

"Liz. I'm tired. We'll talk when you get home. Okay?"

"Sure," I'd said, feeling helpless.

The helpless feeling carried over to the next morning as I stared up at the unfamiliar ceiling, trying to convince myself to get up and go to the hospital.

The message light is flashing on the bedside phone, and I wonder why I hadn't noticed it the night before. I pick up the receiver, punch in a few numbers and listen. It is Grace. She had left the message at five o'clock that morning, and I can't help wondering what she was doing up and so alert at that hour.

I listen groggily as she says that she got my message yesterday and wants to meet me for brunch at ten o'clock. She rattles off the name and address of her favorite diner, and I have to rewind the message and listen to it twice to make sure I get it right.

With two hours to kill, I pull on my sneakers and decide to go for a jog. I don't want to think about Grace. I am already emotionally drained. The added knowing that I am about to see her for the first time in five years makes my nerves feel raw and exposed.

I am excited and sick to my stomach all at once. The last time we'd met hadn't gone very well. But we've kept in touch since then, sporadically over the years, especially since the advent of e-mail. Perhaps all of the tension is behind us. Maybe the past is finally in the past. But our lives have intertwined in the oddest ways since we first met. It is difficult to believe even now that there isn't somehow some significance in our meeting again.

As my feet methodically hit the pavement, I count backward, trying to figure out how long it has been since we were together. The first time. Our versions of the same story were, I knew, dramatically different.

In her mind, I simply dumped her. Crushed her. Devastated her.

In my mind, it was never so easy. Nothing about Grace ever was. She was so young. All sweetness and innocence rolled up together. Those cow-brown eyes would look at me, and I would tremble in their pure honesty. I was never so deserving.

First of all, by then I'd been around the block. More times than I could even count. I was older than she was. Granted, by only five years, but the difference between my twenty-four and her nineteen years could be measured in ways more telling than simply time. I was hard. She was soft. I was cynical. She was trusting. I was raised in a single-parent, blue-collar home where none of the children even dreamed of college. She was born to a family where savings bonds were purchased and safely tucked away as a simple matter of course.

Connie had been gone for three months, and I was having difficulty adjusting to my life without her. I had seen Grace at the bar many times while I was with Connie. I continued to notice her over the several months after Connie left. But Grace and I had never even said a word to each other. We played by all the unspoken rules.

The bar was separated into two specific groups. The older, die-hard dykes kept their distance from the college, preppy crowd.

But I'd noticed Grace, all right. She was about my height, five-four or so, but lankier, leaner. Her hair was cut short, its unruly curls a burnt auburn, with hints of sienna that teased me under the subdued, flashing lights. Across the bar I'd see her clutching a beer bottle to her chest while her throaty laughter reached my ears even at a distance. Over the months we'd gotten to the point where we would make eye contact and give each other a small, barely perceptible nod of recognition. But the rules were the rules, even if they were unspoken, and neither of us crossed that invisible line. So she stayed on her side with her college friends while I continued to stay with mine.

It was on rare occasions that I ventured out to the bar on a weeknight. Rarer still that I wandered in alone. But something drove me out of my apartment on a particularly cold, snowy Wednesday in late November. Only a few lonely souls had braved the cold that night, and Grace was one of them.

As I planted myself on a bar stool, I could see her reflection in the mirror directly before me. She was leaning over the pool table, concentrating on a not-too-difficult shot. I glanced away only long enough to order a drink when the crack of two cue balls colliding reached my ears just before a sharp pain pierced my shoulder. I grabbed my arm, wondering what had hit me, and found a splatter of blue chalk along the length of my sleeve. Curious, I glanced at the floor beside me, and sure enough, the offending blue cube lay just at my feet. Bending to retrieve it, I raised my eyes and found Grace staring at me, eyes as big as the cue balls themselves as embarrassment colored her thin features. She was horrified.

She was gripping a pool stick with both hands and cringing with apology. I couldn't help the grin that I know was plastered on my face as I covered the few feet between us.

"I am so sorry," she was saying. It was the first time I'd heard her speak, and my senses were already taking in the sound of her voice.

"I believe this belongs to you," I grinned as I held out my hand, the small blue cube resting in my palm.

"I'm so sorry," she repeated, her cheeks a rosy crimson as she grew even more embarrassed. "I hit the ball too hard," she spoke quickly, trying to explain. "It bounced and hit the chalk, and the chalk just flew across the room."

I didn't care what she was saying. I was just glad that she was talking to me and that the ice was finally broken.

It was weeks before we kissed. Months before we made love. Even though I wanted her badly, I held off, heart all aflutter like a schoolgirl. Which, I reminded myself often, she was. Every look, every touch, every word she spoke was filled with adoring love. She treated me with a gentle sweetness that I had never known. While I, in turn, held her in extreme reverence. I reveled in her love, all the while knowing that it wouldn't, couldn't last.

But Grace reached me in ways that others hadn't even touched. She softened my hard edges and made me want to give as I had never given before. I wanted to hold her, protect her, and keep her safe from the world. But at the same time, I had come to understand for the first time in my life what it meant to be in a different social class.

I never felt adequate. Grace was so bright, so quick. And while she seemed unaware of our differences at the time, I believed that sooner or later she'd figure it out. Sooner or later I would no longer be able to hold her interest. Grace was headed for big things, and I believed that I would never fit into her adult life.

Grace and I had been seeing each other for nearly a year when out of the blue Connie called. She had finally settled down in Los Angeles and wanted me to join her.

Somehow, I made my heart go cold enough to walk away from Grace. Regret came quickly, moving into my heart and taking up residence in my life. Thirteen years later the regret still hadn't left me.

I broke into a full run as memories from that time threatened me.

Connie and I lived together for the following year, but we weren't exactly lovers. We realized within a month that whatever we'd felt in the past had fizzled. What happened after that was convoluted now, and no longer clear in my memory.

A year after I'd moved away, I called Grace on a whim. We met in Miami, where we spent the most incredible week of my life together. We admitted our mistakes. We cried. We made love. We planned our future. Grace was going to join me in Los Angeles, where we would finally be together. I was on top of the world. For about three months.

She stopped calling. She avoided my phone calls and stopped sending me letters. For days and then weeks I was frantic and sick with worry. It took months before reality sank in.

In the meantime, Connie moved home to Champaign. I eventually learned from Connie that she and Grace had met and had a brief affair.

I have never before or since felt so betrayed. The blow was so cutting that the injury felt physical. I was in a stupor for months, blindly stumbling through each day for nearly a year. Until I met Joanna. In so many ways, she saved me and helped me to believe in life and love again. That happiness was possible.

In the years since, my encounters with Grace have been limited to two brief visits when she'd come to the coast. We share an occasional e-mail about politics, topics of the day, or gossip about an old friend. And Christmas cards. Every year we exchange cards. The annual rite that I love and hate all at once.

My pace slows as I near the hotel, and I double over when I can't suck enough air into my lungs. *"Damn,"* I swear, hating the tide of memories that continues to sweep over me. My breathing finally slows and I look around, squinting into the sunlight.

A mixture of dread and anticipation is gurgling in my stomach. And I know that the racing of my heart has nothing to do with the fact that I've been running.

Chapter 4

As I slide into a booth I can't help smiling to myself as I glance around. When Grace had said to meet her at a diner, I envisioned the old dilapidated type I'd grown used to during my childhood. This is no diner. It is an upscale, hi-tech restaurant fashioned with art deco and a shiny metallic and neon decor. I suppose I should have known better.

My eyes keep darting nervously to the door, looking for the familiar features. I almost don't recognize her at first. All I see are the red business skirt and jacket. The controlled yet tousled auburn hair cascading to her shoulders. The quick, impatient glances thrown around the dining area as her eyes move from table to table, searching me out.

Then the hostess is upon her, smiling a greeting and catching her attention. A broad smile spreads across Grace's features, and a faint buzz begins around me as heads turn to stare at Grace.

She continues to smile as she banters with the hostess. I stare, barely breathing as I will her to look my way. Her chin lifts, brown eyes meeting mine above the hostess's shoulder. I know I am imagining the way she seems to stop moving for the slightest moment as recognition registers.

Then she is thanking the hostess and nodding in my direction before stepping away and walking toward me. I don't know whether to stand or sit. An eternity passes as she makes her way to me. Enough time that a rush of thoughts and emotions race through my mind. Excitement. Nervousness. The anxiety is nearly overwhelming.

I don't know what I'd expected, but it certainly wasn't this. The last time I'd seen Grace, her hair had been cropped short. She'd worn T-shirts and jeans. Maybe an occasional oxford shirt. Every day. I had never seen her in a skirt. Certainly not a short business suit that hugged her thighs so closely.

The once-short auburn hair is now long. Copper locks fall across her brow, framing high cheekbones and falling below her shoulders. A thick gold necklace scoops her neckline. Two large gold and pearl earrings hug her ears. And makeup. She is wearing makeup. My god, she looks straight. Or at least like a Republican.

All these thoughts in the few seconds it takes her

to reach me. I suck in my breath, hoping that she won't notice how difficult it is for me to keep my smile from crumbling.

Awkwardly, I stand to receive her quick shoulder hug. Then she is sliding into the booth across from me, her smile brilliant, and I find myself staring into those eyes. Those cow-brown eyes that have always melted me so easily. After all this time, here I am staring into Grace's eyes again.

"Hi," she begins brightly, the smile never leaving her face. "I'm so glad you were able to meet me."

"Me too." Breathless, I feel like I am staring far too long. "You look great. Really wonderful."

"Well, thank you." She accepts the compliment and brushes it aside quickly, but politely. "How's Connie?" Her features soften and the smile vanishes as she grows serious. A waitress appears, greeting Grace by name and anxiously pouring coffee for the both of us.

"Not good." The waitress disappears and Grace turns her full attention back to me. "She broke her neck. She's still in a coma."

Grace's lips purse together tightly. "What are the doctors saying? Did you talk to her family? Did you find out how it happened?" The questions come quickly, leaving no room for reply.

"Whoa," I laugh. "I can tell you're in the news business. You sound like a reporter," I tease.

She responds by lifting one side of her mouth, chagrined. "Sorry."

"That's okay." Our conversation pauses awkwardly as the waitress reappears to take our order. Again the waitress hovers, practically fawning all over Grace. Once she disappears, Grace turns her eyes back to mine and I color guiltily. She'd caught me staring, assessing her.

"You were telling me about Connie," she reminds me, and I fill her in on what I know.

"She's in pretty bad shape." Images of Connie's swollen features refuse to leave my mind. I shudder and Grace reaches across the table to touch my forearm, urging me on. She lets me talk without interruption for some time, her brows pulling together as she listens intently.

"My god." Grace shakes her head as I finally grow quiet. "It's so hard to believe. I mean, we see things like this happen every day, but I've never actually *known* someone . . ." Her voice trails off. "How's her family doing?"

I shrug. "Okay, I suppose. I met Connie's lover yesterday. I'm not sure that her family likes her much, and she seems possessive. But I think I'd probably like her if I got a chance to know her." I begin telling her what I knew about Wendy, until the waitress appears again and our conversation moves on to more general topics.

"So how's work going?" I ask, groping for neutral conversation. What I really want to do is ask why she dumped me so many years before. I want her to finally explain to me what had gone through her mind and why she stopped returning my calls.

"Very well, actually. What about you? You said in your last e-mail that you were thinking of leaving advertising."

"I did it." I nod, feeling both proud and foolish at the same time. "I quit."

She stares at me, brown eyes wide. "You quit?" I can tell that she is struggling with how to react.

Grace is, after all, a very practical person. "Are you working? Do you have another job?"

"Kind of."

The look on her face tells me she thinks I'm crazy.

"I'm freelancing right now. Photo shoots. Print ads. That sort of thing. I did an assignment last month for a local magazine that I'm hoping will pan out."

She continues to stare, not quite getting it. "Isn't that what you were doing at the advertising agency?"

I nod and try to explain. "Yes and no. I just got tired of being on someone else's clock and working on assignments that someone else wanted me to do." I shrug. "So I quit." My voice sounds nonchalant as I speak, hiding the fact that I'd agonized for months before finally gaining the courage to step out on my own.

"So what does Joanna think about it?"

I'm impressed that she remembers Joanna's name. "She's very supportive."

Grace nods slowly, her smile unwavering, not quite reaching her eyes. I am beginning to feel like she is just going through the motions, asking the polite questions. "And how's that going? You and Joanna."

I smile, uncertain how to reply. How honest did I want to be? "Good," I finally say. "I'm very fortunate. We just celebrated our ten-year anniversary."

Her face falls, momentarily wistful. "Wow. That's incredible, Liz. Congratulations." Her expression is earnest. "Really. That's great." The soft huskiness of her voice begins stirring memories.

I am surprised by the depth of her sincerity and

have mixed emotions. I had expected to feel a certain triumph in being able to tell her that I was in a long-term relationship. Instead I feel hollow. I suddenly want to tell her the truth. That the relationship has been over for three years. That we just decided to split up. But I bite my tongue. Grace isn't a best friend with whom I can talk and share my deepest feelings. She is an ex-lover. For whom even today I still have feelings. Pride will never let me tell her the truth.

"Thanks." I mumble the word uncomfortably. "What about you? Are you still with —" *Damn! I'd forgotten her name!*

"Dana," she supplies the name smoothly. "No. Not really." She shrugs her shoulders, suddenly far away. "We don't really see each other much anymore. She has her work. I have mine..." She lets the sentence drift off, and I find myself surprised by her honesty.

The waitress comes by, interrupting again and asking Grace if she needs anything else. "Just the check, please." Grace smiles sweetly, her business voice trilling.

I wait until the waitress is out of earshot before cocking my head to one side and grinning. "They treat you like royalty here. Do you come here every day or something?"

Her cheeks grow a light shade of crimson, and her lashes drift downward. "I guess. Something like that." Her smile is nearly bashful, and for a brief instant I am reminded of the Grace of fifteen years ago. The one who looked at me so shyly and without guile. She'd been so innocent back then.

The spell is broken as she glances at her watch and nearly jumps out of her seat. "Damn. I'm running late." Her brow furrows. "I hate to do this, but I have to go."

I stand up just in time to receive her hug. "I'm really sorry. Do you mind picking this up? Next time we'll have dinner on me, okay?" Her smile is brilliant as she steps away briskly.

A moment later she is gone, the sound of her heels on the tiled flooring echoing in my ears. I fight the urge to run after her and ask when I'll be able to collect that dinner. Foolishly, I want something concrete. Something to hold on to.

As I drive back to the hotel, I feel my emotions swinging back and forth. It was so good to see Grace, and yet so depressing.

Once back in my room, I flip on the television and quickly scan the channels, looking for the local news. Channel Thirteen has that weatherman that I recognized from many years before. He's aged rather nicely, I decide, before turning up the volume and pulling my suitcase out and tossing it on the bed.

I pack slowly, my mind jumping back and forth between my meeting with Grace and the visit to the hospital that I am planning. I decide I will spend the afternoon there, hoping for a change in Connie's condition before I have to get to the airport.

I can hear the weatherman bantering enthusiastically with the news anchor. But I am so focused on my plans for the day that it takes me several moments before the voice begins sinking in. It is familiar. Husky. That throaty laughter that I'd recognize anywhere.

I straighten up and turn slowly toward the television screen. My senses know what to expect, my eyes and ears transferring a humming sensation all the way down my spine. I glimpse the red jacket. The copper tresses and those brown eyes that had stared into mine just half an hour before.

"In other news today, fire officials are focusing on arson as a possible cause for a three-alarm blaze that occurred overnight in the downtown district. Here with an update on that story is Jim Craig."

The picture flashes to a young, fair-haired reporter standing before a pile of smoldering black ash. "Thank you, Grace. Fire officials do, indeed, believe that a three-alarm fire..."

I hear no more. My ears are humming and my knees can no longer hold my weight. With a loud *oomph*, I collapse on the bed, my jaw slack as I stare emptily at the television screen.

"She's the fucking news anchor." I say these words aloud, my eyes never leaving Jim's features. "No wonder everyone was fawning all over her. She's a fucking celebrity."

Chapter 5

Hopelessness hangs in the air of Connie's room. Even Wendy seems vulnerable, her brows pulling together with worry as she watches over her lover. I stay just long enough to give my phone number to Charlene and ask her to call me when Connie's condition changes. Then I head to the airport and board the first available flight.

That evening, I curl up next to Joanna on the couch and tell her all about my weekend. She knows me so well, and she understands my fears about Connie. We talk openly about the possibility of

Connie's death and about the possibility of paralysis even if she survives.

Joanna understands, too, that it isn't just the fact that Connie is lying in a hospital bed that has me so upset. She knows that part of it has to do with my sudden acknowledgment of the fragility of life. She also knows that I am feeling guilty for losing touch with Connie. That I regret not working out some of our differences over the past few years.

She knows that Connie and I had argued. That a wedge had been forced between us. What she doesn't know is that the wedge was named Grace. Joanna doesn't know that I have blamed Connie all these years for my failure with Grace. Even though I really know it had nothing to do with Connie, I have blamed her because I needed a reason. Because Grace had been completely absent and unreachable, Connie became the easy target.

I had been wrong to take it all out on Connie. And earlier that day I had wanted nothing more than for her to open her eyes so that I could tell her.

Joanna's arms are a warm, safe place. As I thank her for listening to me, I touch her lips with mine and arousal stirs inside me. Refusing to let the fear of rejection find its usual place in my mind, I let my hands wander over Joanna as my mouth opens for her kiss.

But none comes.

"Kiss me, honey," I whisper, and she does. But the lips pressed against mine are unyielding. Her teeth are clamped firmly together, and I break away from the kiss in frustration.

"What's wrong?"

"Liz, we shouldn't do this." Her voice is quiet yet firm, and I feel suddenly like a child being chastised.

"I know." Embarrassed, I drop my head.

"You're just emotional right now," she says.

"I know," I agree. "But it's not just about Connie. I think it finally hit me over the last couple of days that you and I aren't going to be together any more."

She stares at me, eyes sad. "Me, too. But we both know it's time."

I nod in full agreement. Then I study her features closely. "Are you seeing someone else?"

Her jaw drops, and she looks like I've slapped her.

"No. Of course not. You know better than that." I did. I knew she would never have an affair, and she would never see someone else without telling me.

"Oh, I know." I tell her. I study her features, tracing the lines of her face that I know so well. Something inside me gives a little, and I know that as difficult as it may be, it's finally time to let go.

I wrinkle my nose and cock my head to one side. "It ain't gonna be so easy, is it?" I ask rhetorically.

"Nope." She shakes her head. "I love you, Liz." Her voice catches a bit.

"I love you, too." And I do. I've never doubted it for a moment. Not the same kind of love that brought us together ten years ago, but genuine all the same. My heart melts and I pull her to me, wrapping my arms around her and holding her as close as I can.

* * * * *

Wednesday morning I meet with the editor of *City Magazine*, a Los Angeles–based magazine that focuses on the glamour of L.A. life. It is a trendy magazine that features articles on L.A.'s finest restaurants, famous nightspots, and local nontourist attractions. I had done a photo layout for them a month before on Los Angeles nightlife. It had been my very first magazine assignment that didn't have anything to do with an advertisement, and I was anxious to see the final layout.

The meeting with Christine Walters, the editor-in-chief, is brief. While I wait for her in her office, I browse through one of the current issues and blink hard when my eyes focus on my very own photographs.

"Nice, huh?"

Feeling like I've been caught with my hand in the cookie jar, I jump up and drop the magazine to the coffee table.

Christine laughs, her long slender fingers retrieving the magazine I'd just dropped.

"Go ahead. Look again. They're great photos. The layout is far better than we'd expected." She flips through several pages and places the magazine back in my hands.

"Really?" I accept the magazine and study the images, a smile on my face.

"Really. Don't sound so surprised. They're fabulous." She slides into the chair behind her desk and faces me squarely. "We want you to do more."

I have known Christine for many years on a strictly professional level. We first met when my agency did some advertising work in *City Magazine.* Over the years, we developed an almost mentoring relationship, as she encouraged me to take more risks with my career.

"What did you have in mind?"

"Kelly Wagner is doing a series of articles over the next few months. The top ten cities in the United States and how they compare to Los Angeles." She pauses briefly, dramatically. "Do you know Kelly?"

I nod. "We've met a few times. Mostly at conferences. That sort of thing."

Christine's nod is curt. "Good. Anyway, we weren't really concerned about the photos that would accompany the article originally. But we've changed our minds. I think it would be an interesting perspective to have similar images captured in each city. Naturally it would make sense to have the same photographer in each location bringing the same focus to each city." She pauses, a tiny smile on her wide mouth. "What do you think?"

I hate traveling. "Sounds like a great idea."

"Are you interested?" Her expression is a mixture of professionalism and minx.

"Of course."

"Good. I'd like you to work with Kelly to develop a schedule. I'm assuming one or two weeks a month for the next six months or so. I want to start the series next month. Are you available?"

She knows that I am. "Absolutely."

"Good," she says again, this time standing and reaching over to shake my hand. I jump to my feet and press my palm to hers.

"I'll give Kelly your number, and I'll have

contracts drawn up and sent over. I want to move quickly on this, so let me know right away if the contract isn't to your liking." Her eyes are practically twinkling as she escorts me to the door, and I know that the contract will be very much to my liking.

On cloud nine when I return home, I dance into my makeshift office and flip on the computer. I sit down as I do each day and log on to the net. Since I haven't checked my e-mail in days, my in-box is stuffed with messages. I scan down the list of return addresses, my eyes settling quickly on a message from GSULLY731. Grace. I check the date with interest. She'd sent the message last night. I click on the message and read.

> Liz —
> Oops. Sorry I left in such a rush this morning that I stuck you with the check. I promise I'll buy dinner the next time you're in Champaign.
>
> Enjoyed our visit. Far too brief, though. It's good to see that you haven't changed a bit. I think maybe I've missed you. Maybe.
> — Grace

I read the message twice before trying to reply. Then, typing her name, I smile to myself as I remember the way that waitress had hovered all over us.

> Grace —
> You were holding out on me. Tsk. Tsk. You didn't

tell me you were a celebrity. And it's not like you
to be so shy. Congratulations. I hope you'll tell me
all about it.

How sweet of you to offer dinner in Champaign.
Particularly when you know that I get there so
often. I look forward to collecting.

I read my words and frown, wondering if I would
come across as silly or as sarcastic and witty as I'd
intended. There is no way of telling, really. I want to
come up with some clever way of letting her know
that I have missed her. Very much, in fact. But wit
evades me. And I don't want to be misinterpreted, so
I decide to keep it simple. Sighing, I continue to
type.

Yes, it was good to see you. I've missed you, too.

Before I can think better of it, I click the send
button and the message is gone. For a moment I sit
in my chair, staring at the screen and thinking about
Grace.

An image of Connie, face swollen and eyes shut,
comes to mind and I shake my head. Connie and
Grace. Grace and Connie.

The phone is ringing. My business line. I pick it
up and use my best professional greeting. Moments
later I place it back in its cradle and do a silent
little dance. Kelly Wagner wants to meet me after
lunch.

Chapter 6

" Hi." That voice. Completely unexpected.

"Grace?" It's only been a week since I saw her, but the sudden knot in my stomach is at least the size of a softball.

"I'm afraid so." Her voice is dry. "What are you doing for lunch?"

"Today?" Caught off guard, I am a bumbling idiot.

"No. Three weeks from tomorrow," she laughs. "Yes, today."

The knot turns to panic. After one week of dueling and flirtatious e-mails, Grace is suddenly here. Today. I glance at my watch. Nine o'clock. "Where are you?"

"At the airport." Her voice is growing clipped, impatient. "I wasn't going to call. But since I'm here I thought I might as well. I'm on my way to a meeting right now but have a few hours to kill before my flight leaves this afternoon. Can you get away? I know it's short notice."

My eyes find my reflection in the mirror above the bureau. My tousled hair is sprouting out in all directions from beneath a backward baseball cap.

Shit. Shit. Shit. "Of course I can get away. Where? When?"

I can hear the sound of paper rattling. "The Pier Plaza hotel in Long Beach. Two o'clock. Okay?"

"I'll be there."

She signs off and I listen as the line goes dead. I'm not sure if it is the phone or my head that is buzzing.

She is sitting in a wingback chair. Only her profile is showing. One slender, nyloned calf is draped over the other, casually bouncing slowly as long fingers tap the arm of the chair. Today the suit is navy, the silk blouse underneath a conservative white. Necklace and earrings are tiny pearls.

As I approach from the left, her chin lifts and comes around until our eyes meet and a broad smile lights her features. She uncrosses her legs and is on her feet to greet me. Our hug is brief and awkward, the heels of Grace's shoes making her several inches taller than I had expected.

"Somehow I don't remember you being so much taller than me." I eye the heels of her pumps and she laughs.

"That's because I only wore sneakers when I knew you before." Her voice drops down to a conspiring whisper as she links one arm through mine and begins walking me to the door.

I feel myself blushing. Uncontrollably and for no reason.

"So where are you taking me to lunch?" she asks sweetly.

"Oh, no, you don't." I stop in my tracks. "It's your turn to buy, remember?" She has continued on at the same pace so that I have to hurry to catch up with her. It is amazing how long her stride is, even in heels.

"No," she is saying, throwing her words over one shoulder. "No. I distinctly recall that my offer was dinner in Champaign." She stops briefly as I catch up with her, a playful smile on her lips. "And we are definitely *not* in Champaign."

"No, we're not. But how about if I settle for lunch in Long Beach and call it even. Deal?"

One eye squints playfully as she considers the proposal. "Oh, all right. Deal. Where am I taking you?"

"Just around the corner," I grin. "Pier Four."

Both eyes narrow now. "Huh. Now why do I think I'd have gotten off cheaper with dinner in Champaign?"

"Please," I continue with our usual banter, referring to the current topic of our e-mails. "Here you are a successful news anchor. A celebrity, no less.

You must be swimming in cash. Surely you can afford a simple luncheon for two."

"Uh-huh." Her voice is thick with a mocking twang. "And you're nothing but a simple picture taker, right?"

I grin, nodding. "A mere pauper."

"Uh-huh."

I laugh and lead her just a few steps down the block before holding open the door and ushering her inside. The ambiance is stunning, and I take note of the appreciative look in Grace's eye.

The maître d' arrives and ushers us to a quiet corner table. Grace orders a bottle of cabernet, and the waiter is filling two glasses within minutes.

"What shall we toast?" I ask.

"Old friends?"

Over the years I have referred to Grace in many ways, both publicly and privately. I've used many euphemisms. *Old friend* is not one of them. In fact, the phrase makes me uneasy. "How about to your success?"

She inclines her head and our glasses clink. I sip gingerly. "So why didn't you ever tell me about being an anchor? I'm so proud of you."

She smiles and shrugs, a combination of nonchalance and bashfulness. "It's a long story."

"So tell me." I really do want to hear how it has come about. "And tell me what you're doing here."

Her face falls just a fraction, and she sips her wine slowly. "I had an interview this morning."

"Here?" If I had just taken a drink, it would have been all over the linen tablecloth at that very moment.

"San Diego, actually. KQTV Channel Five."

I stare at her, unable to control my disbelief.

She returns my stare, smile fading slowly. "Ooh." She clucks her tongue and shakes her head slightly. "Don't get too enthusiastic, Elizabeth. You wouldn't want me to think you might actually enjoy having me so close by." Her sarcasm is heavy, giving away her hurt. Quickly, I try to recover.

"Are you kidding? That's incredible. Fantastic." I am smiling in earnest now, my mind still reeling. "I just can't believe it."

"What, that I might finally leave Illinois? That I might actually be that successful? Or that I was silly enough to think you'd be pleased?" Sarcasm threatens her voice.

"No. Stop it, Grace. It's not that at all." I drop my voice down low as I appraise her. "I never doubted for a moment that you would be successful. I'm not surprised by that at all. It's just —" My lips clamp together tightly as the old pain begins to rise.

"Just what?" Her voice is quiet now, too.

"I just can't believe that you'd consider moving to California. Now. After all these years." I bite my tongue, refusing to say the rest of what I'm thinking. *After all these years. When you were going to move out here all those years ago to be with me.*

"Ah." She watches me silently for a moment, and I'm uncertain whether or not she can see through me. Her tone changes, and though she smiles, her eyes lack the playfulness of moments before. "Well you needn't worry. I doubt that I'll get the job anyway."

I sip my wine, knowing that I'm already drinking

too much on an empty stomach. My heart softens, and I can feel the corner of my mouth pulling upward. "Grace, I'm sure you can pretty much go anywhere you want to. I saw you doing the news. You're good at it. Exceptionally good." I can see the heaviness lifting from her eyes. "But why would you consider leaving Champaign?"

I watch myriad emotions flicker across her features as she drinks her wine slowly. Over the next few minutes, she tells me the story of how she ended up becoming a news anchor. She had started out writing copy for others, and was eventually asked to fill in occasionally for the anchors. She has been doing the morning and noon editions for three years, and had hoped that by now she would be moving up to *prime time*, as she calls it. But the same anchors have been doing the evening news for nearly twenty years, and the station wasn't about to upset their viewers by replacing the aging newscasters with anyone. Even Grace.

"But why San Diego?" I ask as she finishes her story.

She shrugs. "It's more like, why *not* San Diego. It's a bigger market. There's more opportunity. And they're looking for someone." She shrugs again. "Actually, I'm looking at several opportunities on both coasts. But the competition is really fierce."

Her features soften as our salads arrive. It isn't that she has to leave the Midwest, she explains, but she knows that it's time. She's been itching for some time now, and is more than ready to make the move.

Once the salad bowls are removed, we feast on salmon and tuna. I tell her about my new assignment with *City Magazine*, and she seems genuinely excited for me. Finally I feel my nervousness ebb as more wine flows.

She asks again about Joanna, and I respond more truthfully this time, choosing my words carefully.

"She's wonderful. I've been very lucky." I hesitate. "But the truth is that we've decided to split up."

Grace's jaw nearly drops. "Why?"

"I wish I knew," I say honestly. "We're very close. But it's more like a friendship than anything else." I contemplate this internally for a moment. "But it's difficult to know what's fair to expect after ten years. I wonder if all couples slide into that comfortable, passionless place. Maybe it's normal. I don't know." I regret the words as soon as I say them. Talking about Joanna this way seems like betrayal. Shrugging my shoulders, I settle back into the seat behind me.

"I think I know what you mean," Grace muses. "Sometimes I wonder whether or not two people can sustain that passion thing for many years."

My eyebrow raises as she mentions passion, and she scolds me. "I'm not talking about sex. Well, not entirely, anyway. I'm just talking about that flame, that attraction that brings two people together. Know what I mean?"

I am noticing the darkness of her eyes, the curve of her mouth, noting how neither has changed in all these years. Slowly, my head nods. I know exactly what she is talking about. The wine is making my head swim. Reason is leaving me as old emotions rise. It isn't safe to be here with Grace. Talking this way. Seeing her. I know I will pay the price with her haunting memory as soon as she leaves.

I don't care. Grace tells me more about Dana.

About how they gradually grew apart until they decided about a year earlier to date others.

"And?" I dangle the question, not really wanting to know the answer.

"I've dated a few times." She grins. "Nothing serious."

Envy grips me. Not because I want to date other women, but because I want to date Grace. Still. But it is impossible. *Stop it. Stop it. Stop it.* The mantra begins in my head.

The waiter appears again, clearing the table, asking if we need anything else. Grace shoos him away, glancing around at the other tables that have long since emptied.

"I think he wants us to leave."

For the first time, I notice the emptiness around us. "My god, how long have we been here?"

Grace checks her watch, eyes wide when they meet mine. "Three hours. I think I'm going to miss my flight." She pushes herself back from the table, snapping up her purse as she steps away. "Don't go anywhere. I'm going to call the airline."

While she's gone, I feel myself sobering, growing morose. Why hadn't it worked out with Grace before? I couldn't remember anymore. But I am suddenly angry. Angry with myself for letting her go. Angry with her for not wanting me enough. Angry at Connie for fucking Grace. Angry at Connie for getting on that stupid little plane when she should have been driving to the music festival. Angry because the accident caused Grace to call me. Angry because I saw Grace. I don't want to care about Grace any-more. Too many years . . .

She is back, sitting across from me. The smile she

flashes is brilliant. "Yep. I missed it." She sounds like a misbehaving child. "Do you need to go? Or can you stay a while?"

"Of course I can stay." I wouldn't dream of leaving. So I excuse myself to make a phone call and hurriedly call home to leave a message on the machine for Joanna. I tell her where I'm at and who I'm with. Then I realize I have no idea what time Grace is leaving, and say I'm not sure when I'll be home. I hang up the phone guiltily, shaking my head as I return to the table.

Grace has ordered more wine, and I grimace playfully. "I have to drive home," I remind her, then flag down the waiter for some coffee.

We speak briefly about Connie, and I remember that I need to call her mother. Then as the wine begins to wear off just enough that I am beginning to have my wits about me, I take a deep breath of air and spit out the question I have wanted to ask for over ten years.

"What happened, Grace? Back then." The smile falls from her face, but I press on, my voice sounding shaky. "One day it was just over, and we never really talked about it. I never knew why."

Her lips press together, and a crease appears between her eyebrows. "You dumped me, remember?" Her voice holds irony.

I know my face registers shock. "*You* dumped *me*. You stopped writing. You stopped calling. Everything was wonderful in Miami. You were going to move to L.A. so we could be together, and then *boom*." My hand thumps the table with emphasis.

"That's not the way I remember it," she says quietly.

How could she possibly deny what had happened? My eyes narrow as a slow, nervous shiver finds my spine. "I never forgave Connie for sleeping with you." I say the words quietly, tonelessly.

Her face blanches. "That wasn't entirely Connie's fault."

My stomach feels queasy. "What do you mean?"

Grace hesitates, visibly uncomfortable. "We were drunk. We met at some party. I went home with her." Her laugh is harsh. "Hell, I didn't even know her name or who she was until after —" Her eyes meet mine briefly, guiltily. "There were pictures of you. Everywhere. All over her apartment." Her voice grows distant. "I got up and went to the fridge for a Coke. And there was your face. Right on the refrigerator." She throws back her head and gestures to the heavens before turning back to me, grimacing.

I can only stare at her, my mind confused. I had totally misconstrued what had happened. All these years, I had let myself believe that they had shared a long, torrid affair.

"You can't imagine what that moment was like. When I realized who she was and what we had done." She is shaking her head, staring past me. "I puked my guts out. Everywhere. What a mess."

Dazed, I force myself to focus.

"I am so sorry for that, Liz." The eyes boring into mine are level, demanding my attention. "Truly. I was so ashamed."

I want to rail at her and absolve her all at once.

Absolution wins out, and I try to lighten the moment. "You must have shit your pants," I sympathize.

"I did. Can you imagine?" She is almost laughing now, clearly relieved at my response.

But something still troubles me, even after her confession. "But what about before that?" The question comes before I knew I was asking it. "You stopped calling months before you slept with Connie." My voice is quiet, bewildered.

Discomfort resurfaces on her features. "I don't know," she says finally. "I was scared. I wanted to believe that you loved me, but I couldn't. I wanted to believe our love was enough, but I couldn't. I didn't trust you. I just kept remembering how you had dumped me before, and I was convinced that you'd do it again."

My stomach falls again. Months and years of torment and self-recrimination. How could she have not believed me? How could she possibly not know how much I loved her? Wanted her.

"Jesus, Grace." I feel sick.

"I'm not justifying what I did." Her words are clipped, displaying impatience. "I'm just telling you how I felt. You dumped me. Period. You were my first lover. I was so completely in love with you my senior year that nothing else mattered. And then you dumped me. To move to *L* fucking *A*. To be with Connie." The tone in her voice leaves little doubt in my mind that old memories trigger as much pain for her as they do with me. "I never got over that. I couldn't forget it. And I didn't trust that you wouldn't do it again."

Sick. I am sick. Stomach lurching and head

pounding sick. I could cry. Tears of frustration for the years of needless misunderstanding.

"I can't believe it." The words squeak from my lips. "I would have done anything for you. To make things right."

Her features are grim. "We can't change the past, Liz. What happened, happened. You hurt me. I hurt you. We hurt each other."

"Ouch. That sounds so cold."

"It's reality." Her eyes grow steely. "We can't change that."

I know she is right, but my heart freezes at the sound of her words. I am reminded how sharp her tongue can be. My face must register my thoughts, because she is leaning forward, elbows on table, and lowering her voice.

"I'm not trying to be mean, Liz. But it took me a very long time and a whole lot of therapy to get past all of that. I don't want to go back and think about it now."

I nod, swallowing my pride and the questions I want to ask. So many questions. But even if she has the answers, she doesn't want to share them. And maybe I'm better off not knowing.

We stare at each other without speaking, and I am aware only of Grace. Time slips, and I see us sitting at an airport restaurant, in Miami, many years before. It had been the end of our week together, when we'd rekindled the past. We sat at a table in the airport lounge, fingers touching across the Formica. Hating to leave each other. Again. Promising that it wouldn't happen again. Promising we'd be together, make it work somehow.

"I should probably go." Present-day Grace is

speaking, breaking the spell. "Will you take me to the airport? Or should I catch a cab?"

"Of course I'll take you." Torture. Pure torture. But I will stay with her as long as I can.

I joke halfheartedly as she pays our check, and we slip back into an easygoing patter. "I'm afraid this more than makes up for that brunch I stuck you with," she grimaces.

I agree that it does, grinning, and steer her out of the restaurant and back to my car. We take the 405 up to LAX and are nearly silent the entire trip.

I pull the car slowly to the curb, happy for the time we've shared, however short. But sad, reluctant to let her go, even though I have no choice. Have no right. It seems she is always leaving. Has always left. Is it the wine or the heart that is mixing the present with the past?

I lift the parking brake and turn the key in the ignition to cut the engine. All around us are cars, dropping off passengers, picking up others. I am suddenly envious of those who are meeting their friends, their family, and their lovers. Finally, I shift in my seat to meet her gaze, although I don't trust myself. The impact of meeting her eyes hits me squarely in the chest. There is a softness there, a wistfulness. For a moment I glimpse it and allow myself the luxury of believing that maybe, just maybe, she feels it too.

Her smile is small but sincere, barely turning up the corners of her mouth. I have to shut my eyes. Hard. For just a moment. To fight back the feelings.

In that flash of a moment I feel the time fall away again. I believe that if I open my eyes, I'll find us in the front seat of my old 1978 Chevy Camaro.

The one I owned fourteen years ago when we first were dating. If I open my eyes, the woman beside me will be just a kid, her face void of makeup and short, tousled copper locks curling over her brow.

"What are you thinking?" Her voice is soft, husky, breaking my reverie.

I look at her, regret full on my face, I know. "I don't know. Déjà vu. Or something like that."

"I know." Her smile fades as her eyes grow darker.

"It seems like . . ." I know the words, want to say them, but am unwilling to do so.

"Just yesterday," she finishes my thought.

For a moment, unbidden tears nearly erupt. Swallowing hard, I keep them in check. "Exactly," I agree. I'm feeling less alone, validated somehow. We continue to stare, smiles small, insulated from the activity around us.

Finally I see the flash of light on the gold of her watch as she checks the time. "I have to go." The inflection in her voice is nearly a groan.

I nod. The spell is broken. Almost.

I jump from the car and am around on her side before she has a chance to close the door behind her. I stand inches away, looking up at the brown eyes, and a laugh spills from my lips. She quirks an eyebrow, and I point to her heels. She catches the joke and returns my laughter.

Then she reaches out and I step into her arms. Awkwardly. Always awkwardly. But she holds me this time. Close. The length of her body full against mine. Then she is stepping back, removing herself from the embrace, her smile sad as she lifts a hand to wave.

"Thanks for lunch," I say.

She bows a quick *you're welcome.* "I'll e-mail you," she calls, and I nod.

"Take care." I'm waving now, watching as she turns away, her walk brisk as she clutches her purse to her side.

I wrap my arms across my chest, shivering in the cool spring evening. Watching as she goes inside the terminal. Watching until all I can see is the top of her head among the throngs of so many others. Watching until she vanishes from sight. Again.

Chapter 7

I double-click on the Internet icon, impatient as the modem does its negotiating and finally logs me onto the Net. I scan my e-mail, and know I'm smiling as I click on the message from GSULLY731 and read Grace's message.

Liz —
Thanks for joining me yesterday for lunch. I enjoy your company.

I probably shouldn't tell you this, but they say

honesty is the best policy, right? I hadn't expected us to dredge up our past, and I'm sorry that I reacted the way I did. So much happened back then, things I can't really explain, or even understand anymore. But there were moments yesterday, sitting there with you, that were so familiar to me. And in the car, it would have been so easy to lean over and kiss you, just like before. All those years ago.

On the plane, I thought about everything that happened. I think I buried so much back then. I took real, genuine feelings and purposely twisted them into something negative to make it easier for me to let go. I am so, so sorry for that now. I did love you, Liz. Honestly, I did.

I know it's inappropriate for me to say these things to you. But you seemed so confused about what had happened that I thought you deserved an explanation of sorts. I was pretty messed up back then. I'm sorry. And regret, after all these years, that I hurt you. I don't think I ever thought I had the power to hurt you then. I'm sorry.

Anyway, please don't read into what I'm writing. I'm just having a weak moment. (Not something I admit to easily.) We can pretend I never sent this e-mail, okay?

— Grace

p.s.
Picked up *City Magazine* at the airport. Impressive stuff, my dear. You've come a long way from those

pictures you used to take of the old dilapidated
farmhouses. Remember those?

I read the message three times before I believe
that she's actually written the words. I stare and
stare, waiting for my reaction, an emotion of some
sort, and find that I'm stuck between elation and
sadness, carefully not feeling a thing. Her words are
too unexpected. Maybe too late. Maybe I don't believe
them.

I agonize over how to reply for a good twenty
minutes before giving up and typing.

Grace —
I was never very good at pretending, but promise I
won't hold your confession against you. In fact, I'll
even admit that I felt it too, in the car. I'll admit
that it isn't easy to see you, and spend time with
you, without thinking of the past and wondering
why we didn't work out. For the life of me, I don't
understand it, and probably never will. But it was
good to see you. Really. Thanks for the afternoon.

— Liz

p.s.
I love my dilapidated farmhouse photographs.
(Please note that they're referred to as
photographs, and not pictures, now that I'm a
professional.)

I hope I've ended the message with just the right
touch of humor, and quickly send the e-mail before I
can second-guess myself again.

* * * * *

I spend the rest of the day running errands, talking to Kelly Wagner, comparing schedules, and finally agreeing on the first city of our tour. San Francisco. We decide to drive up the coast together in two weeks.

Throughout the day, whenever I catch my mind slipping to Grace's e-mail, I push the thought away. *Focus.* Her words replay in my mind, and I try my hardest to give them no meaning. But I can't help the way my heart sings, or the smile that hovers on my lips. *She felt something.* Unbelievable. Maybe inconsequential. But after all this time, Grace still felt something. I wasn't alone.

That evening, as Joanna and I prepare dinner together, my mind continues to be preoccupied, drifting toward Grace.

When the phone rings during dinner, I nearly jump out of my seat. "Let the machine pick it up," I say, even though I am itching to pick it up. Just in case.

Joanna ignores my suggestion and brings the receiver to her ear.

"Hello?" Her brows pull together as she listens. "Sure. Hold on just a second." She holds the receiver toward me and I take it, wondering if it really could be Grace after all.

"Hello?"

"Elizabeth? It's Mona Kaplan."

"Mrs. Kaplan." I hope the disappointment doesn't show in my voice. "I'm so glad you called. I've been thinking about calling you all week. How's Connie doing? Any change?"

There is a long, drawn-out silence on the other end of the line. "She never woke up, Lizzy. The funeral's on Thursday."

I can feel the top of my head blowing off as a whooshing sound explodes in my ears. I can't breathe. "No. Oh, god." I know I'm talking, but am not sure how. "Oh, god." I'm doubling over now, my heart having slid down into my stomach.

The rest of the conversation is a blur. I know I say I'll be there. That I'll be on the first available flight. I try to find words of comfort before hanging up the phone, but have no idea what I've just said.

Joanna is taking the receiver from my grasp, wrapping her arms around me as I struggle to pull air into my lungs. *"Fuck."*

"Oh, honey." Joanna's voice above the roar in my ears. "I'm so sorry."

"Fuck."

I curl up into the safety of Joanna's embrace, letting her hold me and rock me and tell me that everything will be okay.

Chapter 8

The bruises have disappeared from Connie's face. She is still swollen and puffy, but she's more recognizable to me now than she was three weeks earlier. When she was in the hospital. When she was still alive.

Maybe it's the makeup. Maybe they've covered up the bruises. I am morbidly curious but find that I can't look at her for more than an instant at a time. My eyes dart to her forehead, noting that they've managed to cover the missing patch on the top of her head. And her hair, it's back to its white-blond color. All traces of blood have been washed away.

I've watched Connie sleeping literally hundreds of times in the past. But I still think she looks odd without her glasses. Doesn't anybody else notice? Shouldn't she be wearing her glasses? I know that I'm being irrational. I know that it doesn't matter whether or not she's wearing her glasses. I know that she'll never open her eyes again. But I must find something to focus on. Something to occupy my mind so that I don't have to think anymore about death.

Wendy joins me beside the casket, and my eyes slide to meet hers. Red-rimmed. Her eyes are puffy, and no amount of makeup will hide this fact. She is no longer the proud, stoic woman I met three weeks ago. She is broken. Lost. I already spoke with her earlier in the evening, so I don't speak now. Instead I conjure up a tiny smile, incline my head, and turn to leave her alone with her lover.

I look down at the carpet as I walk down the aisle to the back of the room and find an empty chair. From where I sit, I can see the back of everyone's head as they bow and pray and wipe their eyes and grieve. This is the second time in two days that I have been to the funeral home and am almost past the initial shock of Connie's death.

Now I find myself observing. Observing the oddities and idiosyncrasies of individual behavior that occur only under circumstances such as these. My own behavior, I must admit, included.

I have spoken with Connie's mother, to Charlene, and to Wendy. I have seen and spoken with so many friends from the past that my mind and voice are exhausted. I'm overwhelmed but numb. Going through the motions. Watching the events that surround me as if I'm not really here.

Tomorrow is the funeral. Finally. I don't think I can possibly take any more. Joanna says that what I'm experiencing is a normal reaction, but I'm not so sure. I've gone from feeling the gut-wrenching, soul-searing pain when I first got the news, to intense emptiness and regret, to my current state of cold, detached emptiness.

A loud sob reaches my ears from the front of the room. Wendy is crumbling now, and a small pain pierces my heart. Hyperventilation is threatening, so I step through the curtained doorway to my right and head for the lobby and the door that allows my escape. The spring air is brisk, and I breathe it in deeply, relishing it. Embracing it.

When I arrive back at my hotel, the thought of being alone in my room sends me straight to the hotel bar. It's nearly empty, so I prop myself up on a bar stool and order a gin and tonic.

Before the bartender can pour the drink, I feel a presence beside me. I know without looking that it is Grace.

"Hi." She greets me quietly, her voice caressing the syllable. "Are you still mad at me?"

I haven't looked at her yet, am afraid to, actually. So I wait until the bartender returns with my drink. Wait until he recognizes and greets her. Wait while he gushes on and on and asks what it is he can get her.

"A glass of cabernet, please," is her reply. He scampers to pour a glass, filling it far too full, and places it on the bar in front of her.

"On the house," he winks. I know he wants to chat, so I muster up what I hope is a most withering look and throw it his way. Grace remains a virtue of charm.

The bartender gets my hint and reluctantly slithers away. Grace picks up her glass and lifts it to her lips as she repeats the words she'd spoken earlier for my ears only.

"Are you still mad at me?"

I steel myself against her, against feeling anything, and risk a glance at her eyes. I'm completely disarmed.

She is referring to a brief conversation we'd shared two days earlier, when I'd called to let her know about Connie. I had told her that the funeral was Thursday morning and asked if she'd like to go with me. Her response had been a cross between a guffaw and a chortle. "I'm not going to the funeral," she stated simply, as if it were the most ridiculous suggestion she'd ever heard.

I was appalled, and during the next minute or so, I gleaned that she was somehow afraid that she would be outed if she showed up at Connie's funeral. She was a high-profile public figure, she explained, and how would it look if she attended the funeral of some lesbian who'd died on her way to the Women's Music Festival. I told her that I personally didn't give a shit what it would look like, to which replied that it must be very easy for me to fly in on my shiny white horse, be the concerned and grieving ex-lover, and then blow out of town again. She, on the other hand, had to stay.

I'd hung up the phone feeling more shaken than when I'd first called her. I damned her silently and wondered how she could possibly be so callous.

Now I choose not to answer her question, but to pose one of my own. "How did you find me?"

"I know a lot of people in high places," she smiles. But when it becomes clear that I'm not in a jovial mood, her smile fades and her face becomes clear and earnest. "I followed you."

It takes me a moment to understand. "From the funeral home?" I'm incredulous.

She is nodding, unashamed. "Look," she begins. "You hung up the other day without giving me a chance to explain." She pauses briefly, all traces of her smile vanishing as her eyes pierce mine. "I don't mean to sound cruel, Liz. But I barely knew Connie. She was *your* lover. She was part of *your* life, not mine. I met her just one night. Other than that, the only way she ever touched my life was in a negative way, through you. So if I can feel any pain right now it's over *your* loss. Not mine."

I take a moment to digest her words and know that she is right, no matter how difficult the honesty is to hear. Her eyes are searching mine, becoming wary. "I know I made it sound like I was only worried about being outed the other day. But that really isn't the issue for me here. I've made no attempt to hide the fact that I'm gay. I was just using that as an excuse the other day. The truth is that I'm just not comfortable with going to the funeral, okay? Please just respect that."

Part of me understands. Part of me doesn't.

Grace continues to stare at me another moment, misinterpreting my lack of response before averting her gaze and reaching for her wine. "Christ," she mutters. "I barely even recognized her."

Confused, I raise a brow. "You saw her?"

"Yesterday morning," she tells me quietly, her eyes focusing somewhere behind the bar. "I was there briefly."

"At the funeral home?"

She is rolling her eyes in my direction, and I can tell that she knows I don't believe her. She tosses back the rest of her wine and turns back to face me, her lips a tight, straight line. "Look," she begins brusquely. "We can't talk here. Can we go up to your room?"

"Sure." I slide from the bar stool and lead the way to the elevators, wishing with every step that I could shake the fog that surrounds me.

Chapter 9

"You're right," I tell her, finding a lame smile. We are in my hotel room. While Grace has settled down in the only comfortable lounging chair, I've dropped down without ceremony onto the bed. "Sometimes the past gets jumbled in my mind. I forget that you two didn't really know each other." I can feel the crease growing between my brows.

"It's funny. You two are so interconnected in my past," I muse, lifting a finger to smooth the crease. "Sometimes I don't know what was real and what wasn't."

Grace is watching me, her face softening.

"I mean, clearly what was real for me wasn't necessarily real for you. We both remember it so differently."

She grins a little, eyes dancing. "You mean like how you keep insisting that I broke your heart when you know it was really you who broke mine?" Her smile is crooked, and I am suddenly reminded of who she is, what she has been to me, and the impossibility that we are here together. After all these years.

I return her smile, although her statement is less than amusing and only adds to my sadness. "Something like that," I tell her. "For so long now, I've thought that you and Connie had this long, passionate affair."

"She didn't tell you the truth?" Grace's frown reappeared.

"I don't think I ever let her." I could still remember the phone conversation. When Connie had blurted out the words *I slept with Grace*, the telephone had literally slipped from my hands and fallen to the floor. My lungs had filled with a sudden, leaden weight as glittering spots erupted behind my eyes.

"I don't want to hear another word," I had said when I was able. "I can't fucking believe you're telling me this, Connie," I'd spat.

"I thought you should know."

"I don't want to know anything about you and Grace fucking," I screamed. "How could you do this to me? Why are you telling me this?" I was blind with seething. "To gloat? Is that it?"

"Of course not, Liz. I —"

"No more," I interrupted. "I don't want to hear any more."

Before she could utter another word, I slammed the receiver onto its cradle and sank to the floor, fighting the nausea that overtook me.

It was several weeks before Connie and I spoke again. Our relationship became strained and distant from that moment on. And she never mentioned Grace's name again.

I recount the story briefly to Grace now, leaving out the part about how much it had devastated me.

She is leaning forward, eyes narrowing as her elbows come to rest above the knees of her jeans. "You have to let go of all of that, Liz. You can't keep feeling guilty for things that happened over ten years ago."

"I know that," I tell her. "I just need to sort it out."

She shakes her head. "You think too much."

I'm not sure if she is kidding or not. "I know that, too." My smile is satiric, until an image of Connie's face, amid the soft pink pillows of the casket she now lies in, comes quickly to mind. Tears threaten to spring. "I just wish I'd known. I've blamed her all this time." I wince, mentally kicking myself.

Grace moves forward, moving from chair to bed in a single movement. "Hey." Her voice holds that quiet sweetness that jars my memories. She lays a casual hand on my outstretched leg. "Stop doing this to yourself. Let it go."

I hear her words, but they don't register. All I see is Grace's unsmiling face, dark eyes intent on mine. She is trying to comfort me, and I'm struck by this fact. I realize in that moment that she is the only lover from my past that has not made the transition to friend. I've only been comforted by Grace the lover, never as Grace the ex-lover. I don't know how to take it, how to react. But I know as I look at her that we will never be friends.

I continue to stare, my mind thrown back in time to that first year. Before she'd grown up. Before cynicism had crept into her voice and into her heart. Before her eyes had grown scornful. Before her laugh had grown mocking. Before her wit had become cutting. She had comforted me often then. In the sweet adoring way that was so exclusively hers.

I remember her e-mail now, remember the mentioned kiss, and my eyes fall to her mouth. Such a kissable mouth.

"Why didn't you blame me?" she asks, breaking through my reverie.

It's my turn to smile. "Don't get me wrong. I blamed you for plenty," I assure her.

Grace rewards me with her throaty laughter.

"But never for what happened with Connie." I grew serious again.

"But why?"

I hesitate and grow nervous, knowing my reply, not wanting to let her see the emotions behind it. "Because I loved you," I sigh. "Because in my mind you were so pure. So sweet."

A wide, mischievous grin slides across her face. "We both know that's not entirely true, don't we?" Her eyebrows are dancing wickedly, and I laugh. My mind races, wondering if she's insinuating that she isn't so sweet and pure, or that she doesn't believe my reason for not blaming her. I assume the first.

"You were sweet to me," I remind her, then reconsider. "At first."

"Ooh." She cringes. "And pure?"

More images flood my mind, quick, staccato flashes. Grace in Miami, her body smooth with sweat beneath mine.

Now my grin is as wicked as hers is. "Virginal."

Her laughter is delicious.

"Okay," I admit. "Maybe not. But before, yes. The first year." My smile softens as I watch her digest this. She is thinking back, remembering.

"You were my first lover, you know." She says these words as if they hurt her, and I feel my heart constrict. Regret. So much regret. Regret that has haunted me for years.

"I'm sorry I hurt you." I've never meant the words more.

"I know," she assures me.

I want to take her hand, step into a time machine, and go back to that time of innocence. I want to take it all back and start over, knowing then what I know now. It takes everything inside me not to say these words aloud.

"What made you come here tonight?" I ask instead. "Why did you track me down and follow me?" It's my turn to watch her shift with discomfort.

"I'm not sure . . ." Her voice trails off slightly. "I think I began to panic, a little. It seems like we've been in touch so much lately. Like you're somehow part of my life again." She was at loose ends, searching for words. "I was afraid that after tomorrow you would leave and that would be it. Poof. Out of my life again."

My eyes close briefly, involuntarily. She has been reading my mind, echoing my thoughts.

"We're always leaving each other." Her smile is sad, reaching her eyes. "I've missed you. And I don't want to lose you again, Liz."

"Grace." Her name leaves my lips as I shake my head, checking my words. "You just don't know," I say finally. Then before I know it, my arms are reaching out and Grace Sullivan is moving into them, the palms of her hands pressing against my back as my fingers find the length of her curls.

I'm astonished as my mind begins to scream. One month ago the idea of holding Grace like this was inconceivable. But here she is, holding me close.

Moments pass as I listen to our quickened breathing. We are unmoving, awkward together, and I know this moment is as much a shock to her as it is to me.

But as our breathing settles, I begin to feel her fingertips roll along my spine. I bury my face in the nape of her neck and breathe deeply, remembering her scent, memorizing the feel of her smooth skin against my cheek.

Joanna comes to mind, and I push the thought of her aside. Forcefully. Purposely. There will be plenty of time to think about Joanna later, I know. At this moment all I know, all I care about, is that I am holding Grace Sullivan in my arms.

My lips brush her throat. Once. Just once, I tell myself. Then her lips are traveling my neck, my cheek. Our breath mingles and becomes labored as our mouths move closer, each of us asking the other the same question. We hesitate as our lips finally meet. Tentative. So tentative. Gentle and unsure. But soon there is the certainty as our mouths remember. Heads tilt just so while lips part and the sweetness of her tongue finds mine.

I shudder as our breathing becomes so loud that I can hear nothing else. Hands are moving now, fingers touching, tracing lines along skin that until now was just a memory. Remembering.

The kiss is broken, and we pull apart from each other, just enough for our eyes to meet as we catch our breath. I expect to find laughter in her eyes, a sort of triumph. Instead I see a seriousness that sobers me. My heart turns over at least three times, and I wonder if I ever stopped loving Grace Sullivan, even for one moment of my life.

Her lips turn down at the corners while her nostrils flare slightly from her effort to calm her breathing. Dark eyes dart back and forth between mine, looking for an answer.

"I should go," she says, finding her voice.

I know she should leave now. But I'm not ready for the moment to be over. Not yet. Maybe not ever.

"Please don't." The words are out before I'm even aware of it. "I don't want you to go."

Again, the triumphant smile that I expect to see on her face does not appear. Instead, her frown begins to soften and a heavy sigh escapes her lips as she wraps her arms around me and pulls me close again.

Chapter 10

Slowly, I become aware of sunlight spreading its heat across my cheek and I turn my head away from the brightness, blinking the sleep from my eyes.

"Is it really you?" Grace's voice is husky with the morning, her eyes twinkling with something between mischief and disbelief. She is propped up on one elbow, the stark white sheet covering her body from the shoulder down. She is grinning as she lifts a finger and lets it trace the line of my chin.

"Hi," I smile sleepily. "So I wasn't dreaming after

all." My arm reaches out and curls behind her head automatically.

"Who had time to dream?" Her chuckle is low. "We didn't even sleep, did we?"

I stretch and purr as she leans over me, her mouth beginning to play along my collarbone. Every muscle in my body is sore with pleasure, and I tell her so.

"You're just out of practice, sweetie," she whispers against my ear, not knowing just how accurate a statement she is making.

"Does it show?" I ask her, feeling a momentary flash of inadequacy.

"Absolutely not." She shifts her weight until her full length is on mine. My arms slide up and come to rest around her neck.

I return her smile, making a game of tangling my legs with hers. She is staring down at me, brown eyes wide. My fingers fall to her mouth and I want nothing else in the world but those lips to cover mine. Again.

"I don't think I've ever kissed anyone for so long," I muse, and lift my head just enough to press my lips to hers.

"Mmm," she sighs. "That was wonderful."

I can't deny it. We had spent hours just kissing and touching, reacquainting ourselves with each other.

Now I look up at her, remembering our passion, still not quite believing that Grace is here in my arms. "I'd forgotten how incredible it is with you."

"Really?"

I think about it only briefly. "No. That's not true. I don't think I've ever forgotten." Our eyes meet and lock, speaking volumes about all things between us. All things past and now present.

"How long will you be here in town?" she finally asks, breaking the spell. "Do you have to go back right away?"

I sober at her words, remembering why I'm here. Remembering the mess that I know will probably greet me when I get home. I'm not ready to go.

"No. I can stay a while longer." I reach up to brush aside a stray curl from her forehead. "How long did you have in mind?"

Her eyes sear into mine again. "I suppose forever would be out of the question?"

My heart does flip-flops even as I watch her cringe at her own words. "I'm sorry," she says. "I shouldn't have said that."

"Shh." I put my finger to her lips. "Don't be sorry." I can feel unreasonable tears trying to squeeze from beneath my eyelids. "Please don't be sorry." My lips replace the finger on her lips, and we are kissing in earnest now, our bodies stretching with hunger as hands and fingers and tongues grow more and more demanding.

Chapter 11

Grace just barely jumped out of bed in time to shower and run to the studio. I am lying exactly as she left me, curled up in the oversize bed, while I watch her report the morning news.

Her hair is pulled back and twisted in a fashionable knot. Her cheeks are flushed and her voice even huskier than usual. For the first time in my life, I feel desire from an image on the television set. She is nothing short of hot. And the knowledge that she has just left our bed, and that we will be sharing another bed that night, makes me want her all the more. I find myself regretting that I won't be able to watch the news at noon.

I take my time showering and dressing for the funeral. My life has taken such a dramatic turn, and I am caught between euphoria and trepidation. I have no idea where this weekend with Grace is leading. I have no idea if it is even leading anywhere. But I don't care. All I know is that she is taking tomorrow off. That she will pick me up at the agency where I'd rented my car at three o'clock today. That she will make reservations at a hotel in Chicago. That we have three more nights together. What happens after that is unimportant to me. Today. But I know that once Sunday arrives I will be fraught with anxiety.

I choose to ignore the warning bells in my head. Instead I methodically change my airline reservations. Then I call Joanne and calmly explain that I am staying until Sunday. She asks no questions. I volunteer no answers.

I do two things that afternoon at the funeral service that cause me immediate shame, which I admit to no one. The first is that I am completely distracted by the time I arrive at the service. I feel myself grow impatient to be gone and away from the cloud of pain and death that has hovered over me since I'd first heard about Connie's accident.

The simpler truth is that I want to be with Grace. Time is now suddenly a commodity to me, and I want to spend every possible moment with her.

As a result I hang back, observing, and find that I am seeing the proceedings as I imagined Grace might see them.

She is correct in her assumption that nearly everyone in attendance is gay or lesbian. I file this information away, imagining that I will tell her she was right. I already know her reply. I know that I will get that I-told-you-so grin.

The second thing I do that afternoon is nonchalantly flip through the guest book, assuming that I'll never find Grace's signature. But there it is, on the bottom of page two, the bold strokes of her handwriting. I am instantly repentant for thinking the worst of her, and reprimand myself immediately for thinking she'd been lying to me.

I stay no longer at the funeral than is socially required. Grace is waiting for me in the parking lot of the rental agency where I'd rented my car. She is impatiently tapping her fingers along the steering wheel of her MG while her eyes scan page after page of the most recent *Time* magazine.

As I approach her car, she lifts her face, revealing dark glasses and a bright, jaunty smile. "Get in," she tells me, her voice hovering between intimacy and lust.

She practically throws the car into gear, and we fly to the highway. Four miles later, she is pulling over to the shoulder of the two-lane road, cutting the engine, and twisting in her seat until her mouth finds and covers mine hungrily. Greedily.

"I missed you," she growls.

"I love watching you do the news." I can barely get the words out around our kisses.

"I couldn't stop thinking about you." Her hands are inside my shirt, reaching up to cover my breasts.

"I was lying in bed, watching you." The throbbing between my legs is unbearable. "Wanting you." Our mouths are open, our kisses anything but soft.

"I want you now." One hand is reaching for the

zipper of my pants. Then I know nothing, feel nothing, except the exquisite pleasure of Grace's mouth and hands.

We are giggling like schoolgirls. The top of the convertible is down, the wind is whipping our faces, and we are laughing.

"And here I thought you were so worried about being outed," I call out. "What if we had been caught?"

"Who cares," she laughs carelessly, grinning as she squeezes my hand. "I'm so glad you can stay." She brings my hand to her lips and kisses two knuckles.

Her smile grows serious for a moment, and she lets her eyes wander from the road to my face. "How was the funeral? Are you okay?"

I shrug and nod at the same time.

"Do you want to talk about it?" she asks.

"Later," I say, curling my fingers around hers. It's too soon to switch back to the funeral and the topic of death. Right now I just want to look at Grace and revel in the moment.

Chapter 12

It is Sunday morning. The day we have both dreaded. The day we have completely avoided. As if by ignoring its looming presence it might pass us by, completely unnoticed.

I feel her beside me before I open my eyes. She is watching me, lying on her side, elbow propping herself up as her chin rests in the palm of one hand.

Her eyes are dark. Nearly black.

She is crying. Silent tears swell and spill down each cheek and drop to the pillow below. I can't help notice that the path is well marked from tears before.

My throat constricts and tightens. I recall the last time I saw her in tears. In the Miami airport. When she'd held me and we'd sobbed uncontrollably. *Always at an airport. Always saying good-bye.*

"I don't want to lose you again." She chokes out the words. I know how rare it is to get this close, for her to let anyone in. Her voice caresses me, soothes me. Seduces me.

"You won't, Grace," I whisper. "Please believe that."

"You don't understand," she says. But I do. I've never understood anything more in my life. What I can't believe is that she is giving voice to the very emotions I am feeling.

"Understand what?"

Her jaw sets tightly as she gains momentary control of the tears. I watch the struggle play across her features, and my heart swells as I watch this proud, stubborn woman.

"I love you, Liz." She isn't smiling. "It's that simple for me." The words leave her lips in a whoosh. She hesitates briefly. "You're the woman I want to be with. Whatever it takes. I still want the puppy and the white picket fence. And I still want those things with you."

I cannot believe that I am hearing these words from her lips. I cannot believe she's expressing the same dreams we had shared so many years ago. After all the times I've thought of Grace throughout my life. After so much regret.

I don't know whether to laugh or cry. But my heart begins to cave inside my chest, and the vision of her brown eyes, hovering inches above mine, begins to blur as tears win out over laughter.

"Grace," I say. "I don't think I ever stopped loving you." I blink hard and wipe the back of my hand across my eyes. "Don't get me wrong," I begin to sniffle. "I haven't been pining away or anything. But you've always been right here." I tap my chest above my heart, and she places the palm of her hand in that very spot. Her smile is wistful. "Like a constant reminder of what I once had. And what I once lost." I think about never seeing Grace again. Never touching her. Never kissing her. The tears begin in earnest.

"I don't want to lose you either, Grace. Not after we found each other again. That would be too cruel." I shake my head. "Never again. Never."

She gathers me up in her arms and I bury my face in the hollow of her neck. "I love you. I've always loved you." I whisper the words and she returns them to me, lovingly, adoringly.

"Promise me we'll get through this."

"I promise."

"Promise me we'll be together."

"I promise."

We won't make the same mistakes again. We promise. This time will be different. We promise. We've learned from the past and won't let anything get in our way. This time we will be together. For certain. We promise.

Chapter 13

Joanna's car is in the driveway when I finally arrive home. I sit in my car longer than necessary, looking up at the house, then out at the vegetable garden that is already overdue for spring planting. I expect to feel something. Anything. Guilt. Remorse. Loss. But I feel only a strange detachment.

What will I say to Joanna? It is the first moment that I've allowed myself to think forward to the consequences of the last few days. Will I crumble the moment I see her? Should I tell her right away?

I let these thoughts circle my brain as I close my

eyes briefly, squeezing them tight. I can see Grace's face if I close my eyes. Her smile brilliant. Wide and toothy with laughter. Then I recall her face as we'd left each other's arms just hours before at the airport. Her brown eyes dark with intensity as the tears subsided and she grew solemn and urgent in her plea. "Don't forget."

"I promise." I'd tried my best to reassure her. Then the flight attendant was calling for all passengers, and I had to leave her.

Grace is still too close to me, her physical presence too clear. My lips are bruised and chapped from hours upon hours of kissing. And even now I want more. Want that mouth on mine with an insatiable hunger that I cannot satisfy.

I finally step from the car, retrieve both bags, and fling one over my shoulder as I make my way to the door.

Silence greets me first, followed quickly by the sound of Ginger and MaryAnn purring with delight as they wind figure eights between my legs.

"Anybody home?" I call out into the silence as I make my way down the hallway to the bedroom.

"In the kitchen," is the faintly distracted reply. I utter a loud *harrumph* and dump my bags to the floor. I can't help thinking that in the old days Joanna would have greeted me eagerly at the door.

"Things sure have changed," I mutter aloud, then cringe a little as I catch my reflection in the wall mirror. "That's an understatement," I tell myself before taking a deep breath and heading down the hallway.

Joanna is sitting at the kitchen table, her attention focused on a notebook computer propped up in front of her. As I enter the room, she glances up and smiles sweetly.

"Hi." She holds out a hand, and I reach out to take it. Bending over, I receive the quick kiss she lands on my cheek before dropping down in the chair across from her.

"How are you holding up?" She wrinkles her freckled nose as she inspects my features. "Was it awful?"

"The funeral?" I ask stupidly.

She only nods. "The funeral. Connie's family. Seeing old friends." She stares at me closely, eyes narrowing. "I can't believe you stayed longer than you had to."

It is my turn to stare at Joanna while I search for a reply. "I needed to stay. I needed to work through some things."

Joanna nods again. "Well, I'm glad you're home. The kitties and I missed you."

I find myself staring at Joanna, thinking about the day we'd adopted the kittens. I wonder for the umpteenth time how it is that we've spent nearly every day of the last ten years together, only to drift apart. I don't know if I even know her anymore.

"We need to talk." The words spill from my lips, jolting me as much as they do her. These are the same words I always utter when trying to broach the topic of "us."

"Do you really think now is a good time?" She doesn't blink. "You just got home. It's been a stressful week."

I realize that she thinks I want to talk about us again, and I hesitate before continuing. "I need to talk to you."

I am suddenly worried. Worried because I know we'd agreed to split up, but it is really too soon to be seeing someone else. Even if the relationship had been over for years. I don't know how she will react to what I have to say.

My mind fast forwards, and I see ourselves explaining to friends. I know how our situation will be interpreted. I was the one who'd stepped outside the relationship. I would be the bad guy. It would be my fault. For the briefest of moments, I hated Joanna for this fact. Then I soften instantly. Contrite. Sad. I had really believed that my life was as close to perfect as it could possibly be. Now I don't know anything. Except that I won't let go of Grace. Not this time. Not after finding her again.

"Joanna," I begin, my voice calm. "Seriously."

She holds up both hands to silence me. "Jesus, Liz. You just got home. You're stressed. Let's talk about this later."

Exasperated, I spit out the words. "Joanna. I'm seeing someone else."

Her stare is level. Her lips a careful straight line. "You certainly didn't waste any time," she says dryly.

Finally, the moment arrives when I hate myself. "Joanna. I didn't plan this. I swear. I had no idea this was going to happen."

An odd glint enters her eye as she appraises me. "I can't believe there's someone else already. How long have you been seeing her? I assume it's a her." She says the last part sarcastically.

"You know better," I quip, recognizing the bitterness in her tone.

"Joanna. You know that I have been completely

invested in this relationship for ten years. I didn't expect this. Honestly."

She regards me closely before snapping the notebook shut. "Are you just trying to get a rise out of me?"

My jaw drops, astonished. I'm appalled that she can think I am making this up just to get a reaction out of her.

"You can't be serious," I say.

Her face registers a number of different emotions before settling, becoming wounded. "There really is someone else?" she asks.

I nod slowly.

"So is it someone I know? Do I want to know who it is?"

I am tongue-tied as I watch a multitude of emotions flurry across her face. Then her face opens, eyelids drawing back as something close to recognition comes over her.

"Grace Sullivan."

I am floored. Completely. Dumbfounded, I simply return her stare.

"Grace Sullivan." She repeats the name again, then begins alternately nodding and shaking her head. "Am I right?"

I swallow hard. "Yes." The word is barely audible. "How did you know?"

"I don't know whether to be angry or worried." Her lips are twisted in a sardonic, know-it-all smile.

"What's that supposed to mean?" I am defensive.

"That I'm not surprised." Her smile fades and her eyes cloud. "You never let her go."

As we stare at each other, I find myself thinking

back to our beginning. Joanna had rescued me from myself. From the pain of losing Grace.

I suddenly feel quite small.

"I'm not going to tell you that this doesn't hurt, Liz. And I'm certainly not about to give you my blessing." She pauses. "Yet." Her sigh is loud as she frowns. "Just be careful, Liz. She hurt you so badly before. Have you forgotten?"

I shake my head. Joanna's words are like a dose of reality. "You fell apart. Literally." She reaches out and covers my hand with hers. "How can you trust her?"

"She explained everything to me. We've talked." I am defensive, my words sounding lame even to my own ears.

"Uh-huh." Her smile glitters, but she is not happy. "Just be careful, sweetie. Watch your heart." She sighs again, this time sadly, and shakes her head. "Not to mention your back," she adds, her voice full of irony.

I search my mind for a quick and cutting reply. Something to defend Grace and our sudden twist of fate. But I come up empty. Joanne is out of the room before I can respond.

Chapter 14

"I can't believe she hasn't said anything lately. Maybe she's realized what she's losing and is changing her mind." Grace looks serious, and I consider the possibility briefly before discarding the idea.

It is three months later, and we are seated in a rather noisy restaurant in the middle of the French

Quarter of New Orleans. This is the fourth of twelve cities that I will be traveling to on assignment for *City Magazine*. Grace has so far met me in each city, and we've managed to plan minivacations around each of my assignments.

We are both uncomfortable with the boisterous crowd, particularly because we are trying to have a serious conversation. But it is our first night in the city, and we quickly discover that the Cajun cooking in this restaurant is nothing short of heaven.

I had been reluctant to talk to Grace about Joanna and probably wouldn't have raised the topic if she hadn't asked. But our relationship has grown deeply, quickly. We talk on the phone at least once a day, often sharing long-drawn-out conversations late into the night. It was during these conversations that I found myself captivated by her all over again. Grace is highly skilled in the art of verbal tennis. She takes the art of conversation to a whole new level, volleying words with wit, charm, and cynicism that are nothing short of exquisite. She is highly intelligent, and has the ability to retain and regurgitate every bit of information that has ever passed her way. Conversations often turn into debates, which either turn dry and whimsical, or heated and competitive. I am wildly attracted to her way with words.

But what I really enjoy the most is when Grace shares a verbal dance. Unlike the volley, the dance is a sharing, a give-and-take. A hinting, a subtle flirting, a spoken batted eye. Her words and her voice caress and render me powerless with such ease. Seduction has never been so tantalizing, so mesmerizing, as it has always been with Grace.

Throughout the days there is a constant, steady stream of voice mail messages and e-mail correspondence. Grace isn't bashful with her messages. They are often filled with vivid descriptions of what she would like to be doing to my body at that very moment. Or if her mood is romantic, she sends a quick note echoing the same wonder I am feeling myself, that we found each other again. And when she is too busy to dally over long, romantic messages, she simply calls and breathes the words *I love you* in a message that I listen to over and over again before finally deleting it to make room for others.

We are constantly figuring out how we can see each other more frequently over the next several months. We go over my schedule time and again as she rearranges her life so that she can meet me. A few days in New Orleans. San Francisco and Miami the month before. Nearly a week in New York City next month. Then Boston and D.C. before heading south again to Atlanta.

Joanna, on the other hand, is acting as though nothing has changed. And in many ways, nothing has. Our relationship is exactly the same as it was before I'd started seeing Grace again. It is a bit strained, perhaps. She doesn't ask about Grace, and I don't mention her name.

"Maybe," I finally concede. "But I don't think so." Joanna had been very clear that our relationship is over.

"It's possible," Grace offers again. "Sometimes it just takes a while for us to realize our mistakes."

"You wouldn't be referring to you and me, would you?"

"Probably," she sighs, and we stare at each other for some time. Both of our smiles falter, and I know that she is thinking about our past. No matter how much our relationship is now and in the present, our past somehow hovers between us from time to time. And with it the inevitable doubt and worry.

"Maybe we should talk about this when it's quieter and we can hear each other." Grace seems to sense my thoughts, and I gratefully nod my head.

We spend the rest of the evening making gluttons of ourselves with food and drink, until at last we can't possibly eat another bite.

"What would you like to do now?" We are leaning over the table, two cups of coffee between us. "See the sights? Go for a walk —"

"Hold you." She says the words softly, yet her voice commands my attention. My eyes are riveted on hers, and I feel the current running between us. Passion. Running slow and sweet down my spine before finding my belly and bursting alive.

Her expression smolders between desire and tenderness, and I'm surprised by the physical response the look evokes from my body. My chest begins to swell and I'm nearly overwhelmed with a sense of joy. I'm astounded once again that we have found each other.

Once we're alone, I sit down on the edge of the bed and pull Grace forward until she is standing between my legs. Wrapping my arms around her waist, I bury my face in her breasts and breathe deeply. Intoxicated, I revel in the feel of her fingers trailing up and down my back as she nuzzles the top of my head.

"I think I have some good news."

Distracted by my growing desire, I mumble a reply and wait for a response. When none comes, I lift my head and look up at her downturned face. She hesitates before dropping down to her knees so that we are now eye to eye.

"Tell me," I smile, but can't resist dropping a quick kiss on her mouth.

"Mmm." Her expression shifts as she leans in for another kiss.

I groan in reply, greedy for her kisses, and gently push her away, smiling. "Tell me your good news."

Her eyelids are heavy with desire as she pouts sweetly. Then the fog lifts and she is focused. "My agent called this morning." Her pause is dramatic. "KQTV offered me the weekend anchor job."

KQTV. San Diego. My mind slides into fast forward, already thinking about logistics. *She'll be less than an hour away. What about Joanna?*

"Maybe it's not such good news?" Grace is cringing, holding her breath, and I realize I haven't reacted to her news at all.

"Are you kidding? This is fabulous. Honey, it's so exciting." I hug her tightly. "You'll be so close."

"It will change our relationship," she says with trepidation. She sounds childlike. Fear is in her voice.

"I'll get to see you every day instead of once a month." My hands rise and cover both of her cheeks as our eyes touch and search out the answer to so many unasked questions. "I thought that's what we both wanted."

"Are you sure?" Her voice is small, quiet.

"Of course I'm sure. Honey, this is perfect. We'll have a chance to really plan a future now. Did you accept the job?" I ask as an afterthought.

"Not yet. I told them I'd be in touch when I get back home."

I can feel my eyebrows pulling together. "Should you wait? Should you call tomorrow?"

"Maybe," she shrugs restlessly. "I wanted to spend a few days with you first. I wanted to talk to you and see how you felt about it before I gave them an answer."

"Are you sure you just didn't want to see whether or not you'd still like me?" I'm teasing her, but know there is just an ounce of truth, and of fear, in my question.

"That's it." Her voice dips into a sarcastic drawl as she raises a carefully plucked brow. "I thought I'd come down to New Orleans and try you on for a couple of days. You know, to see if we can still stand to be around each other after a day or two." She is smiling. But it is definitely a steely smile.

"Hmm. I bet we don't last a night." My voice drops down, becoming seductive as my hands grasp her hips.

"I'm not worried about the nights, sweetie." Her voice is husky as she slides her hands beneath my shirt and traces the outline of nipples with her fingertips.

Our mouths are open and our tongues dancing before either of us can speak another word.

Chapter 15

I don't think that I've ever been this happy. At least it's not the kind of happiness I've felt before. This is different. This is a soaring heart. This is looking into another pair of eyes and believing for the first time that maybe there's something to all of this soul mate crap after all. Maybe I didn't believe it before because I'd never felt this way for another human being. But I believe it now. I believe that she and I are meant to be together.

Leaving her at the airport is not easy. Although she has stopped crying when we part, I cannot help the tears that inevitably spring forth from my eyes. I know that it's silly. Particularly when she chides me. But I can't help the feeling of loss when she walks away from me. And it takes me some time to realize that I don't trust her yet. I don't trust the situation, and am waiting for her to pull the rug out from under me. I know how dangerous these insecurities can become. I know I need to shake them.

The next month is busy with change. I finally move out of the bedroom that I've been sharing with Joanna for ten years. Even though the change is long overdue, and even though not so much as our toes have touched in several years, it is a dramatic and powerful move. The kittens howl their displeasure, even if we cannot, as they prowl back and forth between our separate bedrooms.

Grace and I have begun making tentative plans for the future. She accepted the position in San Diego, and will take two months to make the transition. The television station in Champaign has already begun making counter-offers, and the stress is beginning to show in Grace. I try my best to be sympathetic and understanding while trying to help plan her move.

"I can live anywhere," I tell her late one night as we discuss whether I should stay put while she adjusts or if we should find a place together right away.

"I mean, it doesn't matter if I'm based out of L.A. or San Diego."

Grace seems preoccupied, and I'm not sure if she is listening or not. But I've been combing the Sunday *Times* for hours, trying to find an apartment in the right location.

"Honey?" When she doesn't reply, I prompt her again. "Are you there? What do you think?"

"Oh, I don't know," she sighs, and I feel a prickling sensation along my neck.

Patiently, I try to explain. "I just need to know whether to look for a one- or a two-bedroom apartment."

"Two," she replies briskly, her business voice in evidence. "Either way. Two."

I hate that she sounds so distracted, hate that I can't quite get through to her. But I know I'm being unreasonable and overly sensitive. I am still stinging from Joanna's reaction when she'd learned that Grace was moving.

"I'll believe it when I see it," she'd scoffed. "I'm still betting she stays put."

Even though I'd defended Grace, Joanna's words fed the nagging doubt in my mind. But I know that my fears are irrational. So I keep reminding myself of the tremendous stress Grace is under and that it will all soon be over.

"Okay, honey." I make my voice light. "I'll look for two." I hesitate before deciding to sign off. "Get some sleep. I'll see you tomorrow." I was flying out first thing in the morning for New York. "What time will you be in?"

"My flight gets in at four. I'll meet you at the hotel. Did you get tickets for the show?"

"Yep," I say, enthusiastic. "Wednesday night."

"I thought it was Thursday."

I check my memory. "Honey, you said you were leaving on Thursday."

There is a pause. A hesitation. "Oops. I was going to surprise you. I changed my plans. I'm staying with you all week." She drops her voice seductively. "I didn't think you'd mind."

I chuckle in spite of myself, and feel the glow spread through my limbs. "I can't wait. See you tomorrow."

"Good night, Liz. I love you."

"I love you, too. Bye."

I eye the phone for a moment or two, pushing away the fear that I know is unreasonable. Finally, I pick up my camera bag and begin checking my equipment.

Chapter 16

It is late. I am waiting in a hotel room in New York City. Grace should have been here two hours ago and I am extremely anxious. Agitated. And nearly starving.

Finally there is a knock at the door and she greets me with a long, tired hug that lasts a full minute.

"I've missed you," she whispers in my ear, and I can feel the tenseness in the muscles of her back.

"Sorry I'm so late." She kisses me earnestly before picking up her bags and dumping them unceremoniously inside the room. "Have you been here long?" She is throwing open the closet doors and kicking off her pumps. "I'm starved. Do you mind if we just order room service?"

"Sounds good to me." I smile and retreat to the bed, where I lounge back and watch her unpack and change her clothes.

We discuss what to order for dinner, and I place the call while I wait for her to join me on the bed.

When she lies down and pulls me into her arms, I note that her hips are pointier than usual. "You've lost weight," I tell her, and begin to rub the muscles of her arms. "You've been a wreck lately."

"The last few weeks have been tough," she admits, and I notice the darkness beneath her eyes. "But it's good to see you. I hate it when we're apart."

I smile and touch her lips briefly with mine.

She closes her eyes and hesitates briefly. "Honey, I need to tell you something."

I don't like the sound of her voice. I remain quiet as I search her face for some clue.

"Liz. Honey. I don't want you to get upset, okay?" Naturally, my stomach lurches and I am instantly upset. I realize that I am holding my breath.

I stare at her, unblinking, and hear the strain in her voice.

"I'm going to meet with some people at a local station here in New York on Friday."

My stomach lurches in earnest now, and while I am no longer holding my breath, I find that I cannot breathe.

"They saw some of my tapes a couple of months

ago and have been talking to my agent. They've been trying to get me to interview for the past month and I kept saying no because I'd already committed to you and San Diego." She stops talking, but it's too late. I feel my wall lifting, falling into place. I can't talk even if I want to.

"When I told my agent that I was going to be here this week he convinced me that I should just talk to these guys. So I said okay. It's no big deal, Liz. Honest."

I am quiet, digesting her words.

"Honey?" She lifts her head enough to meet my eyes.

"What if they offer you the job?" My voice is dead.

"They won't." She sounds certain. "And anyway, I'm not interested."

"Is that why you've been so preoccupied lately?"

She looks at me quizzically, then her lips curve in a small smile. "Have I sounded preoccupied?"

"Yes," I say quietly.

"Oh, honey. I'm sorry." Her voice caresses, soothes me. "I've been a wreck. I've wanted to talk to you about it, but I knew you'd be upset. I decided to wait until I saw you."

I am trying hard to trust her. But I can't understand why she would accept an interview if she didn't want the job. I ask her this, and her response comes slowly.

"Professional courtesy, I suppose. It's a small industry and everyone knows each other. I'd hate to ruin a potential situation in the future by refusing to do a simple interview."

It made sense, and yet I didn't like it. "Is that why you changed your plans? Because you have an interview on Friday?"

"That" she rolls over on her side to face me, letting her fingers trace my hairline — "and because I wanted to spend more time with you."

I am suddenly scared to death. "Are you going to move to New York?"

"No!" She is adamant as she wraps her arms around me and pulls me close. "No, honey. I'm not moving to New York." She presses kisses across my cheek and over my forehead. "I'm going to San Diego, Liz. To be with you. We promised each other. Remember?"

Of course I remember, and I tell her so. She continues to shush me with kisses, coaxing first a smile from my lips and then arousal from my body. She makes love to me slowly, gently. As though she is listening to my body for the very first time.

We lie exhausted in each other's arms just as our room service is delivered. Then we eat dinner leisurely and make love again and again until dawn.

This is my very first trip to New York City. I have never felt so out of place in my entire life. Grace, on the other hand, is in her element. The differences between us have never been so evident.

I am constantly lost and out of sorts, and have to rely on Grace to handle almost everything. She hails cabs, gets us seated at restaurants, knows exactly when to tip and how much to give. She absolutely thrives. I am very nearly miserable.

As the week progresses, I begin to feel less of a country bumpkin but am still less than comfortable in the city. As each day passes and Friday looms, my anxiety continues to grow. And while we don't discuss it, it is always there between us.

We make plans for the weekend to drive up the coast to New England, and the week can't pass quickly enough for me.

On Friday morning I'm a wreck when Grace leaves early, dressed to kill in the navy suit. I am thankful for the last-minute errands that I need to run. Thankful that I have something to keep me busy while I wait for her to return.

She is smiling when she opens the door, and she immediately begins the ritual of stripping off nylons and pulling on her jeans.

"Well?" I finally say, knowing that my fear is full on my face.

She pulls a T-shirt over her head and tucks it into her jeans. "It sucked."

She is grinning.

"Really?" I can't help my relief from showing.

"They were a bunch of pretentious assholes." She covers the distance between us and crushes me to her breast. Her lips smack against mine loudly. "You can relax now," she chuckles.

"You're not moving to New York?"

"No." She releases me long enough to pull on a pair of socks and sneakers. "I'm California bound, Missy." Then she pulls me down on the bed and holds me close, gently. Her sigh is heavy. "I'm nervous about moving," she admits.

"You'll be fine. It takes a while to adjust. But you'll be just fine."

"But what about us?"

I lift my head and see the uncertainty in her eyes. "We'll be just fine, too," I tell her.

"What if we screw it up again?"

I'm surprised to hear her talking like this. "We won't let that happen, honey."

"Promise?" she asks, her voice childlike and vulnerable.

"Promise," I assure her.

She considers this, her eyes raking my face before she blinks hard. "Okay," she says simply, stretching. "But do we have to leave tonight? I just want to curl up here with you and plan our future. We can leave in the morning, can't we?"

I smile, heart glowing. "We can stay as long as you like," I say, then feel her breath on my cheek as she curls her body against me.

Chapter 17

At first, when she stops calling, I try my best to give her every benefit of the doubt. After all, she's going through so much right now. She's leaving one job and moving halfway across the country to a strange new place. She is leaving her home of over thirty years and starting a fresh new life.

When she stops returning my phone calls and is vague and evasive when I do catch her, my mind begins to spiral. Déjà vu strikes me hard, and I battle to remember that the past is the past. Grace would never treat me the way she did all those years ago. We've both learned too much from our mistakes in the past. We would never let it happen again. Never.

When she snaps at me, tells me that she's busy and preoccupied, I don't dare venture the questions that I want to ask. She has become a different person. Moody. Unreachable. And while I want nothing more than to be a patient and understanding lover, my inner strength and resolve is crumbling.

Then finally, the truth. But only after I catch her off guard at the studio.

"New York came through with an offer." Her words are cold. Matter-of-fact. My stomach falls below my knees and my head begins to swim. "It's an incredible opportunity. It's the evening news. It's the best market in the entire country and a real springboard to the national news. You know that's what I want, honey." She pauses, but I cannot speak. "I'd be a fool not to take this job."

There it is. The words I'd dreaded but have somehow come to expect. The silence on the line between us is excruciating. Still I can't speak.

"Liz? Are you there?" Her voice is impatient.

"Yes," I manage.

Again the strained silence.

"I can't talk right now. I'm on in five minutes." She sounds exasperated.

"What?" Anger mixes with pain. "That's it? That's all I get?"

"That's all I know."

"Well, what about us?"

"I don't know." Her voice quiets a bit.

"You decide to move to New York and you don't even discuss it with me? Isn't this a decision we should make together?" I'm incredulous. In a state of shock, really. I can't believe this is happening.

There is silence on her end of the line.

"Jesus, Grace. Why haven't you been talking to me about this?"

"I *can't* talk about it," she says simply, as if it is a perfectly reasonable explanation. "Do you think this is easy for me?"

I don't know. I honestly have no idea what she's thinking or feeling or going through, and I tell her so.

Again, silence from the other end of the line.

"So when are you moving to New York?" I ask the question sarcastically, not expecting an answer.

"Next week."

This time the tightening in my throat is overwhelming. *Fuck you, Grace.* I want to say the words. I want to hurt her. I want to take back the power that I've somehow lost. But I don't. I say nothing.

"So it's over. Just like that." My voice is tight, a mixture of sarcasm and unshed tears.

"If you say so," she quips.

Finally, anger washes over me, temporarily overshadowing the pain. "No, Grace. Let's be very clear about it this time. Just so you don't come back ten years from now and try to convince me that it was *me* who dumped *you*. This is *your* choice. *Your* decision. Not mine."

She laughs without humor. "Touché, my dear." She covers the mouthpiece of the phone, and I hear her tell someone that she's on her way. "I need to go, Liz. They're ready for me on the set."

"Fine."

109

There is a slight pause while I wait for her to say good-bye.

"I love you, Liz." Her voice is a whisper.

"Sure." My laugh is obnoxious. "Break a leg, Grace."

"I'll talk to you later. Bye." The dial tone echoes in my ear.

Chapter 18

"Go ahead and say it." I am lying on my make-shift bed, sprawled on my back, arms thrown up to cover my face.

"Say what?" Joanna's voice is soothing.

"I told you so," I say bitterly. I sneak a peek at her face and catch her gentle smile.

"Well, believe me. There's a big part of me that wants to say it. But it wouldn't feel very good." She reaches out and strokes my hair, and for an instant I'm reminded of my mother. It's such a maternal gesture. "It's too obvious how much you're hurting."

Part of me wishes she wasn't being so nice. Instead of soothing me, it only served to make me feel more vulnerable.

"Do you want to talk about it?"

I shake my head. "It doesn't feel right. Talking to you about Grace, I mean."

She considers me closely. "It's okay, Liz. You need to talk to someone. What's going on? Why isn't she moving here?"

I close my eyes briefly, still not believing it. "She got a better offer from a station in New York."

"New York?" Joanna is incredulous.

My reply is a grimace.

"She's moving to New York?" Her voice has lifted a full octave higher than usual.

Again I grimace. "She's already there." I close my eyes again. "I think."

"You *think?*" Her features register shock.

Finally, I meet her eyes and realize that I'm embarrassed. "I haven't talked to her in three weeks."

A low groan starts deep in Joanna's throat, and her face grows a bit pale. "Christ, Liz. Did you fight? How did this happen?"

"No, we didn't fight. It was unexpected. At least to me." My embarrassment grows. "That's not true. Part of me expected it."

Joanna stares at me, dumbfounded. "Liz. This doesn't make any sense. Tell me what happened."

"I don't know. She was all set to move here, and then she got an offer from New York. It's a bigger market and she'd be doing the evening news."

"What would she be doing in San Diego?"

"Morning news. Weekends." I run my hand

through my hair. "The same thing she was doing in Champaign."

"So New York is a big step up." Joanna's voice is normal now.

I nod. "She said she'd be a fool not to take it." For a moment I remember the first time I'd seen her doing the news. The red suit. Pearl earrings. The dazzling smile and the husky voice. My heart hurts at the memory. "And she's right."

Joanna is frowning. "Did she talk to you about it before she accepted the job?"

I wince and shake my head, feeling duped. Or at least a fool.

The skin tightens around her lips. "Did you at least talk about what you're going to do? What your plans are?"

Again I shake my head.

"Jesus, Liz. You talked all the time."

I cringe. "I know. I don't have any answers."

"Did she at least ask you to move out there?"

"No." I remember our trip to New York and smile wryly. "It was pretty obvious that I don't fit in there. You know I'm not exactly a big-city girl."

Joanna considers these words and smiles softly. "That's not necessarily a bad thing, sweetie." She ruffles my head. "That's part of your charm."

"Huh," I grimace.

"What are you going to do?"

"I don't know. I keep going over it and over it. But no matter what I do, I can't reconcile it. It doesn't make sense."

"I hate to say it, Liz. But I don't think this is about you."

"Maybe it's not *about* me, but it sure as hell *affects* me."

"You need to see her. Talk to her."

Guffaw. "Honey" — sarcasm drips — "I don't even have a phone number or an address."

Joanna's eyes narrow. "Your girlfriend is really beginning to piss me off."

I laugh in spite of myself. "I don't think she's my girlfriend anymore," I say, and am totally unprepared for the truth of those words. My throat tightens and tears spill instantly.

"Fuck."

"Oh, Liz." She hugs me briefly. "I just can't believe this."

"Sure you can," I sniff. "You expected it."

"No. Not really. Not like this." She snaps her fingers for emphasis. "I can't believe she would dump you for a job."

I cringe from the honesty of her words. "I guess that speaks pretty loudly, doesn't it? Says a lot about how she really feels about me." My mind drifts as I voice my thoughts out loud. "She was so convincing. I believed her." My eyes focus back on Joanna. "I really did." I shake my head and begin the internal reprimand that had begun the moment Grace had said she was going to New York. "What a fool I was."

Joanna is frowning again. "I'm sure she loves you, Liz."

The words hurt. "I thought so. I really did."

Chapter 19

I am very close to crawling the walls.

For some reason, I keep believing that she will call. Each day when I awake she is my first conscious thought. Even when I try to push her image away and recapture sleep, I cannot. She haunts me. I roll out of bed, pull on my sneakers, and run blindly. Until exhaustion overtakes me and I have to stop.

I pour myself into my work, but find that it can't possibly fill the hours of the day. I paint the house. Build a new shed to replace the one that is falling apart. Plant so many trees, bushes, and flowers that there is no place left to put them. Anything to keep busy. To keep active physically. But it is not enough.

I push myself each day and don't stumble to bed until I know I can sleep. She is my last waking thought, and in my mind she answers all the questions that I have no answers for.

I stopped sending e-mail some time ago, as she hasn't replied in weeks. And I've given up trying to find a listing for her in the phone directory or online.

She has purposely, forcefully, removed herself from my life. Without warning. Without discussion. She could be anywhere. She could be doing anything. And I'd never know it. Our lives are severed. Completely. Totally.

I am furious. Furious that she lied. Furious that I allowed myself to be taken in. Furious that I ever believed for a single minute that she loved me.

I am dismayed. Bewildered. Why did she bother? What was her motive? It makes no sense at all.

I am betrayed. I'd had no reason to trust her to begin with. I'd believed her because I'd wanted to. Not because she'd ever earned it, or deserved it.

But mostly, I'm just hurt. A pain that I hadn't felt in years. A pain that I never thought I would feel again.

Against my better judgment, I get on the plane and head for New York City. It has been three months. Three solid months of silence from Grace. I have felt every possible emotion over that time, and I am finally at a point where I'm almost worried about her.

"Doesn't it make sense that she would have called by now?" Joanna asked one night after dinner. "Maybe something happened. Would anyone know to call you if anything happened to her?"

"I don't know," I tell her, and am suddenly curious about her friends and family. I never met any of them. And I wonder if she ever mentioned anything about us to anyone.

"Have you thought about calling the stations in New York and trying to track her down that way?"

Actually, I have thought about it. Several times. "I think she'd be pissed if I did that."

"Gee," Joanna's voice dips into a sardonic lilt. "I wonder if she worries about your feelings as much as you worry about hers."

I get the point, and am abashed. "You're right. I guess it's beyond that, isn't it?"

Joanna doesn't answer me directly. "Look, Liz. You can't keep up the way you're going. I see how you're pushing yourself. You have to make up your mind that you're not going to give her the power to do this to you anymore. You can't just go through the motions while you wait for her to pick up the phone and call."

"I know you're right," I say, wishing that I had the courage to put Grace behind me, to cut her out of my heart and my life the way she apparently had already cut me out of hers.

"But there's this part of me," I begin, more to myself than to Joanna. "That still believes in her. I know it's silly, but I want to hear it from her. I want to hear from her lips that it was all a lie. That she doesn't love me."

"You're a masochist," she says flatly.

"Probably," I admit.

"Then do something, Liz. Don't just sit here. Take some control. Get on a plane and go track her down. See her face-to-face and get the word from the horse's mouth."

She picks up the phone and drops it in my hands. Then she watches over me as I book the earliest flight that isn't outrageously expensive.

While on the plane, I go over my plan for finding her. I will check into my hotel in the early afternoon. It is Friday, and I am hoping we can spend the weekend together. My first plan is to pick up all of the local newspapers to see if there is a listing or advertisement for the news.

If that doesn't work, I will wait for the local news to come on and flip channels until I find her. And, if for some reason something has happened and she isn't on any channel, I am determined to call all of the local stations until I find her.

But finding Grace once the plane lands couldn't be simpler. Walking out of the terminal and into the bright sunshine, I blink several times at the harshness of the light. My eyes scan the area in search of taxis, and the billboard is practically, ironically, the first thing that my eyes focused on.

Grace. Larger than life. Her face alongside some young, tanned stud, smiling down at the crowd from fifty feet in the air. The slogan beneath their faces is simple and direct. *Grace Sullivan. Mike Daniels. Your News. Tonight. On Nine.*

My stomach clutches and I stop in my tracks. "Jesus," I mutter.

"Get outta the way, lady." A man with far too much hair on his back bumps into me, and I realize I'm standing in everyone's way. So I move to one side and take a deep breath before gathering the courage to look up at the billboard again.

She is gorgeous. Stunning. And I am still in love with her, for absolutely no reason that I can put my finger on. But my heart knows. My gut says it's that simple.

Yet as sure as I am that I love her, I am equally certain now that it is over. I swallow hard to steady myself as I gaze up into those cow-brown eyes, remembering the first time I saw her. When she was just barely a kid and I was the older one. The wiser one. The one who'd been around the block. And now look at her. Larger than life. Sophisticated. Suddenly I understand why she'd walked away from me. How could I ever compete with all this?

My instinct is to get right back on the plane and head home. But after battling with myself for nearly an hour, I decide to stick it out. At least go to see her, say good-bye. There are still some answers that I need to hear. And I know that seeing her one last time is the first step in letting her go.

I know that if I take the time to check in to my hotel I'm liable to lose my nerve. So before I can change my mind, I hail a cab and head directly to the studio.

Chapter 20

The offices of WNYC Channel Nine are nothing short of opulent. They are right off Central Park, which I gather should somehow impress me although I'm not quite sure why.

Security is so tight that it is tedious. When I finally get past three security checkpoints and produce all kinds of identification and finally reach the front desk to inquire after Grace, I feel like I've already been interrogated.

"Do you have an appointment to see her?" the redhead with bright red fingernail polish inquires.

"No. I'm surprising her, actually."

She looks me up and down, and I am suddenly self-conscious of the way I'm dressed. Too casual in my jeans and golf shirt. Suddenly I wish I'd taken the time to go to my hotel and change.

"I'm an old friend from back home," I explain, and flash what I hope is my best aw-shucks smile.

She isn't falling for it. "So she's not expecting you."

"No." I shake my head and try again with the smile.

She seems to make up her mind and reaches for the receiver of the phone in front of her. "I'll call upstairs and let reception know that you're here. What was your name again?"

"Elizabeth Grey."

She scribbles my name on a piece of paper and presses several numbers on the keypad before speaking.

"Sharon. It's security downstairs. I have a Ms. Elizabeth Grey here to see Ms. Sullivan." She pauses and glances up at me. "No, she doesn't." Another pause. "All right. I'll tell her."

She replaces the phone and gives me a steady look. "She will inform Ms. Sullivan that you're here and call back down."

I nod and wait. And wait. And wait. Twenty minutes pass before the phone rings and I finally see a smile on the redhead's lips.

"Ms. Sullivan says to tell you she'll be right down. Please make yourself comfortable." She indicates the chairs to my right and I settle into one, thinking how silly that she didn't offer one until she knew that I was legitimate.

Before I can calm my thudding heart, Grace is there, striding briskly through the lobby, her smile perfect as she approaches me. My eyes fall to the calves of her legs, stretching forward, exposing just a hint of her thigh beneath a short blue skirt.

"Elizabeth," she calls, far too loudly. I stand, knees wobbly, and she is reaching out to me. Her hands are on my shoulders and her cheek brushes mine in that straight-woman hug that I hate so much. "What a surprise this is." Again her words are too loud, and I know she is putting on a show for the redhead and all of the other security personnel around us.

As she steps back, her smile remains intact and I am hopeful. Just for a moment I think that she really is happy to see me. But her eyes give her away. Grace is furious. Seething.

"I hope I'm not bothering you." I decide the best thing to do is play along.

"Not at all. Are you going to be here long? Maybe we could grab a bite to eat." She continues to smile, and I am amazed at how well she is hiding her anger. How well she plays this game.

"That would be nice," I smile demurely and bend to pick up my overnight bag and follow her outside.

As soon as we hit the pavement, I am struggling to keep up with her. "You shouldn't have come here like this." Her voice is barely above a whisper as she wades out into traffic, trying to cross the street. "You can't just show up here out of the blue."

"I would have called if you'd given me your phone number," I say sarcastically, not bothering to lower my voice.

The light changes and Grace steps into the intersection, hurrying across the street and into Central Park. I have no idea where we are going and have given up trying to keep up with her. So I follow a few steps behind her, watching as heads turn to stare after her as recognition dawns on each passerby. Then she finds a bench in a relatively secluded spot and sits down at one end.

I settle down beside her, careful to keep a respectable distance between us.

"What are you doing here, Liz?" Her smile has vanished and she is no longer whispering.

I shift on the bench, pulling one leg up and around so that I'm facing her. I study her profile and realize with a tug of my heart that she hasn't even looked at me since we were in the lobby of her building.

"I was getting worried about you. We haven't talked in so long. I didn't know what happened. If you were all right." I pause briefly, then lower my voice. "I needed to see you, Grace. To talk to you." She doesn't respond, doesn't reply, and I feel the need to fill the silence. "I don't understand what happened, Grace. I thought we were happy. I don't understand how you just cut me out of your life like that." My voice sounds vulnerable, and I struggle to maintain my composure.

She is quiet as she stares straight ahead, avoiding my gaze. "Come on, Liz. You know why. It's how I cope."

I do know this, I realize, and feel oddly comforted by the fact that I really do know her. Very well, in fact.

"And how am I supposed to cope, Grace? I don't know how to do it your way." I search her profile for a sign. Anything. Any emotion. But I'm not reaching her. She's not giving an inch. "Grace, please. I'm dying inside. I'm so lost. I don't know what to do. If I should wait this thing out. If I should move on."

A couple stroll past, turning to putty when they recognize Grace. She turns instantly into celebrity Grace and bestows a smile in return for their acknowledgment.

Once they are out of earshot, I try again to get some kind of response. "Help me out here, Grace. I need you to talk to me."

"I don't have any answers for you, Liz." Her voice is low and husky. Quiet.

"But, honey, I don't get it. Everything was fine, wasn't it? We were happy, weren't we? Please tell me I'm not crazy here."

"You're not crazy." Her voice had gained a dull quality.

"Then tell me what happened."

Her response is silence.

"Grace, please." I hate the sound of my own voice. Hate the vulnerability in it. Hate the vulnerability behind it. "This hurts so much."

Again the silence stretches, and my hurt shifts to frustration before turning to anger.

"I guess what I'm going through is pretty irrelevant to you, isn't it? All that matters to you is you. Your job. Your career. How you're coping. How you're getting through."

I note the muscles in her jaw are working as she stares resolutely ahead.

"I'd really like to know how you do it, Grace. How do you say you love someone one day and then cut her out of your life the next?"

Her eyes close. One, two, three seconds.

"Things change," she says evenly.

"So even your word doesn't mean anything." My voice is cutting.

Her laugh is harsh, brittle. "I don't know why you bothered to come here, Liz. You've obviously got all the answers."

"I had to come up with my own. I certainly wasn't getting any from you." My sarcasm turns to anger. "I can't believe it, Grace. I can't believe you did this to me all over again. Just like before. How could you? You're treating me like some fuck you picked up in a bar one night. We have a history. We've known each other for a long time."

"Oh, for godsakes, Liz." Finally, I'd hit a sore spot. Her eyes are fire as they meet mine. "When are you going to let go of the past?"

"I'm not talking about the past. I'm talking about the future."

"What future, Liz? We live on opposite sides of the country."

"We didn't," I say quietly. "We made plans to live together. You said you loved me. You said you wanted to be with me no matter what it took." I know that I'm whining and hate myself for it.

She avoids my eyes again.

"What happened, Grace?"

"You know what happened. I got a different job."

"And the job is more important than us." I know that I am setting myself up, know that her words will hurt me.

"My career is very important to me," she says through clenched teeth.

"That's obvious," I respond with sarcasm, and she erupts.

"What in the hell do you know about careers, Liz?" Her eyes sear into mine. "You threw yours away."

"Threw it away?" I guffaw. "Threw it away? Is that how you see it? I paid my dues, Grace. I put up with twenty years of that corporate bullshit. I played the game. For what?" I pause long enough to take a deep breath. "I thought it would mean everything to me. But it meant nothing. Zero. So I *chose* to get out and try it on my own."

"Fine. You chose to get out. You had your shot. So you should understand that I want mine."

I lean forward. "You know what, Grace? That's just it. I *do* understand. I *want* you to have your shot." I feel hot tears begin to threaten, and I force them back. "I just want to share it with you."

Her eyes touch mine briefly. "I don't know how to do that."

"So that's it? You don't even want to try? You're just going to throw everything we have away because it suddenly got difficult?"

"I just can't do it, Liz. I can't focus and give my career everything it needs right now and give enough to you at the same time."

I appraise her for a moment or two before I decide she is being absolutely serious. "Grace," I say quietly. "People do it every day. It can be done. If

126

both of us want it enough." I watch her closely. "But I guess that's the key. Both of us have to want it."

She stares at me for some time, face softening, and all I can think about is holding her, kissing that mouth, and running my fingers through the auburn curls.

"God, I miss you." The words are out before I can catch them.

Her face blanches as she stares at me. "I'm sorry, Liz." She glances down at her watch and is instantly distracted. "I need to go. I have to get to makeup before I go on."

A familiar lump is in my throat, and I struggle to choke it back. "I'm staying at the Plaza in Manhattan." The words rush out quickly.

Grace sighs heavily and looks away. "I don't think it's a good idea for us to see each other, Liz."

My heart is aching that dull, strained ache. "Then tell me it's over, Grace. Let me go. I can't go on like this anymore."

"I can't . . ." She stands up and wraps her arms across her chest. "I can't go through this right now."

Heart in my throat, my mind is screaming her name, begging her not to let me go. "Then I guess I'll have to do it," I say, and I know now that it has to be this way. She would never say the words. I draw a long and haggard breath as I stand and toss my overnight bag over one shoulder. "It's over, Grace. I love you. But I have to let go."

We stare at each other for several moments, until I realize that she has no intention of stopping me from walking out of her life. Then I chide myself for thinking even for a moment that she might. After all, she already walked out of my life months ago.

With that knowledge firmly in mind, I turn on my heel and head back the way we came. When I reach the street I don't turn back. I hail a cab and head straight for the airport.

Chapter 21

I go over it and over it in my mind. I had convinced myself that seeing Grace and saying it was over would make the hurt go away. I know now that I must have been delusional.

I replay our conversation over and over in my mind. I think of clever, cutting remarks that I wish I'd said. Parting shots to hurt her as much as her withdrawal from my life had hurt me. I think of things I'd say if I still had the opportunity.

I hope that microphone keeps you warm at night, was my favorite. But I know that her reply would be equally cutting. Equally hurtful. *I've never had any trouble finding someone to keep me warm at night,* she would say. And I'd be crippled again. Impotent.

Then my emotions swing in the opposite direction, and I am like a wailing child who has suffered loss too many times in a very short lifetime.

I rail at Grace and at fate and want to tell her she's a coward. A coward for giving up on us. A coward for not being able to say the words. A coward for making me say the words for her. No responsibility. That's what Grace wants. As if by simply walking away she is no longer responsible for holding my heart in her hands.

But I'm being melodramatic. Love is not a contract, Grace would say. Even though she promised. And I believed her. Trusted her. Against my better judgment.

There is a strange woman in my house when I return home. She is an attractive, waiflike creature with long, thin dark hair. She is leaning over the kitchen sink, filling an ice tray with water, when I open the back door and step into the kitchen.

Her eyes become saucers and I can practically read her mind, her face is so transparent and open.

It takes me a moment, particularly because I am so deep in a fog that it takes my mind a few moments to catch up with my eyes.

"Uh. Hi." I finally manage a smile and drop my bag to the floor when the kittens descend to greet me.

"Hi." Awkwardly, she places the ice tray down on

the counter and smiles shyly, uncertain. "You must be Liz." She wipes a hand on the thin cotton skirt she is wearing and I notice for the first time that her feet are bare.

A woman whom I have never met is standing in my kitchen at nearly midnight, dressed in a flimsy cotton dress of some kind, and making ice cubes. I'm too surprised to react.

She is reaching out to me with the hand she has just wiped on her skirt and I realize she is waiting for a response.

"Yes. I'm Liz." I shake her hand. "And you would be . . . ?" I let the sentence dangle in the air.

"I'm Amy." She smiles, just as Joanna wanders in and nearly drops the bottle of beer she is holding to the floor.

"Liz," she says.

"Joanna," I reply.

We stare at each other, neither knowing quite what to do. Then we both glance at Amy, and I find myself apologizing.

"I'm sorry. I should have called and let you know that I was coming home early."

We spend the next ten minutes apologizing to each other. Amy insists that she should leave, and I insist that she should stay. Joanna says she's sorry and should have told me, and I say it's okay and we'll talk later.

"Don't let me ruin your evening. Please," I say firmly. Then I give both kittens a scratch behind the ear and pick up my bag. "I'm going to turn in, anyway." I say good night and muster as much nonchalance as I can as I head toward my bedroom.

Joanna is barely sixty seconds behind me. She

opens my door and catches me just as I sit down on the bed.

"Liz. I'm so sorry. I didn't want you to find out like this."

"It's okay."

"We met last month. I've wanted to tell you so many times lately, but you've been so hurt and absorbed."

"It's okay," I say again. *Absorbed* is probably an understatement.

"I didn't want to hurt you any more than you were already hurting."

"Joanna." I hold up my hand. "Really. I'm okay with this. I understand. Stop apologizing." My voice is firm, but it has an edge. My exhaustion is showing.

We stare at each other for several moments until Joanna lets out a huge sigh and steps over to sit beside me.

"So why are you back so soon?" She asks the question quietly, and I suddenly want to cry. But I'm done crying. Tired of crying. Numbness settles over me.

"It's over," I tell her simply. "She wouldn't say the words, but it was obvious. So I said them." I shrugged. "There was no point in staying."

I glance at Joanna, and her eyes are watching me closely. "Are you okay?" she asks.

"I will be," I tell her. Even though I don't believe it yet. But of course I will be. Everyone gets through it, eventually.

The silence between us is comforting, and then I remember that Amy is waiting in the other room.

"Amy seems very nice." I smile and hope Joanna knows I'm sincere.

"She is. Very sweet." Joanna colors just a bit.

"Kind of cute, too." I raise an eyebrow, teasing her.

She reaches out to nudge my shoulder before growing serious. "I hope you'll like her, Liz. That you'll get a chance to know her."

"I'm sure I will," I assure her.

First MaryAnn and then Ginger meows their way into the room, and we both watch as they begin rubbing against our legs.

"I guess you and I have a few things we need to work out, huh?" Joanna sounds sad, reluctant.

I nod, knowing that the time has come for us to let go. "Indeed we do." Tears begin to threaten, this time for Joanna instead of Grace. "We'll start tomorrow." I stand up and pull her up from the bed. "Now get out of here. You have a guest to entertain."

She squeezes me tightly. "Thanks, Liz," she whispers, and my eyes begin to mist over as she closes the door behind her.

Chapter 22

Seven years ago, shortly after Joanna and I had bought the house, Joanna had insisted that we build a swing set that her sister's kids could play on. They lived in an apartment at the time, and Joanna wanted them to have a safe place to play.

They played in our yard nearly every day of the summer those first couple of years. But they are older now, in junior high and high school, and we only see them on holidays.

I sit, with a coffee mug in my hands, on one of the two swings now, listening to the birds greeting the morning. I reflect on how things have changed over the years.

I'd believed back then that Joanna and I would be together forever. Now that the relationship is coming to a close, I'm thinking that Joanna is more family to me than the blood relatives back home. I hope we don't lose that. I hope that we can find a way to bridge this time, blend our past with the future, and come out on the other end still part of each other's family.

My thoughts jump to Grace with a thump of my heart, and I wonder how many days, weeks, months will have to pass before I no longer think of her umpteen times each day.

I sip my coffee and watch a robin search the ground for breakfast. I can hear Joanna approaching from behind. Without looking, I know that she has joined me on the swing beside me. But the morning is too young and I'm far too vulnerable to look into her eyes so early.

"Shouldn't you be entertaining your guest?" I ask the question not to be catty, but with sincerity.

She doesn't reply, and I think that maybe she thinks I'm being sarcastic. I turn to quickly reassure her.

But the eyes that meet mine aren't the blue of Joanna's. They're brown. Dark brown. Slightly blood-shot. Definitely tired. My heart stops beating.

"Hi."

I stare for several moments, not trusting my eyes. Then I blink and return my eyes to the robin, which is still hopping in the grass.

"You didn't check in to your hotel." Grace's voice is quiet, almost gravelly.

"No." My voice is small and not yet quite awake.

"You should have known that I'd never be able to stay away if I knew you were there," she is saying. "I went to the hotel right after my broadcast."

"I had no reason to think you would come." My voice is a monotone. "And I couldn't stand the thought of sitting in a hotel room. Waiting. I had to leave."

"I'm sorry, Liz. You caught me so off guard. I was an ass."

My shoulders lift in a shrug. "You'll get no argument from me on that one."

We are silent for a while, and the robin flies away. Unreasonably, I search for something else to focus on. Anything so that I don't have to look at Grace. My coffee mug becomes the center of my universe.

"I think I woke Joanna up. She didn't seem exactly pleased to see me."

I smile a little at this, then try to remember the last time that the two of them had met. Five, maybe six years ago.

"She only gave me a *small* piece of her mind before she told me where you were," Grace continued, piquing my curiosity.

"Really? What did she say?" I risk a glance and watch her stretch her arms up over her head and grasp the ropes of the swing.

"Oh," she begins wryly. "Basically to shit or get off the pot."

Amused, I glance back over my shoulder and see Joanna and Amy sitting out on the balcony of the master bedroom, nearly a hundred yards away. The absurdity strikes my funny bone, and I raise my mug in a mock toast.

Joanna returns the gesture, and I smile before turning back to Grace.

"Who's that with her?" she asks.

"That would be Amy. Her new girlfriend."

Grace whistled low. "Things sure have changed around here. Are you okay?"

"See what you missed in just three months?" I keep my voice light as I continue. "Yeah. I'm okay. A little sad. But okay."

Grace searches my face and then nods and looks away. The silence stretches, and I'm surprised to realize that it is almost companionable and not uncomfortable.

"I think I counted six billboards and eight taxicabs with your face on them. Just between the airport and your office building," I muse. "You really made it, Grace. You should be very proud of yourself."

"Thanks. But it's all so daunting. Not to mention overwhelming and hectic and scary." She slides me a small smile, and for the first time that morning, I feel a crack in my armor. "It hasn't been an easy adjustment," she finally adds, and I think on this, admitting to myself and to her that it probably wasn't.

My mind digests this information, and I begin to think about what it must be like. To be in Grace's shoes. To look up in the sky and see your face plastered there. Smiling. Always smiling.

"Do you ever get sick of smiling?" I ask stupidly.

"Yes," she admits, grinning, knowing exactly what

I'm talking about. The unexpected grin disarms me, and I avert my gaze.

"I subscribed to *City Magazine*."

"Really?" I'm genuinely surprised.

Grace nods. "It was a way of keeping you close, I think." She blinks and interrupts herself. "Without keeping you close, that is. I was being a voyeur into your life, from afar."

"A simple phone call would've probably been an easier way to keep tabs on me."

She doesn't take the bait.

"I've enjoyed your photographs. You seem to be doing pretty well yourself."

I nod. "I suppose so. I've actually gotten a couple of other assignment offers." I think about the two phone calls that I have yet to return, and shake my head. "Guess I should get back to them, huh?" I say this more to myself than to Grace, who twists an eyebrow quizzically.

"I've been preoccupied." My smile is resigned. "I've been having trouble making decisions. Making plans or commitments of any kind." I tip my head back toward the house. "Even with Joanna. Things have changed so much, and she's ready to move on. I've just been reluctant to do anything until I knew for certain what was happening with us." I choke a little and take a sip of coffee.

Grace bends down, runs a hand through the grass before plucking a blade and examining it closely. "I know what you mean. I haven't let myself think about anything but work. Partly because I want to do well. But also because it can all be so intimidating. Sometimes it makes me want to put my tail between my legs and go home to Champaign where I belong."

Selfishly, I am hurt that it doesn't even occur to her to run to me. Then I realize that it isn't even in her makeup to run to someone. She would rather build up her walls, put her head down, and run full steam ahead. Needing someone was a weakness to Grace, and she would never admit to being so vulnerable.

As if reading my thoughts, Grace's voice drops down to a monotone. "I've trained myself pretty well over the years. I know how to focus. How to shut out every distraction."

"How to avoid things . . ." I smile and am rewarded with a small crinkle at the corner of her eyes.

"How to avoid things." She repeats my words and chuckles.

"You're a master at avoidance," I tease.

"Agreed. But it tends to get me in the end. Eventually." She sighs, growing serious. "I'm sorry I avoided you, Liz. I'm sorry I didn't call. I know it was wrong of me. I knew it at the time. But I've been paralyzed. Cold and paralyzed."

"I would have understood," I tell her.

"And I know that, Liz. But it wasn't about you and me. It was about my career."

I listen to her words and try my best to appreciate them, but I can't. "But Grace, that's where you and I are different. To me it's all the same thing. Everything in either of our lives had to do with us. *Your* career and *your* future had everything to do with *our* future."

She stares at me, and I know I'm not getting through. "Your decision to take the job in New York didn't just affect you. It affected me. It affected us."

Her lips turn down slightly as I continue. "I don't want to start preaching about what I think a relationship should be. But to me it's about making decisions together. It's about building a life together. It's not about saying *I love you* until something comes along that throws a wrench into the works. It's about trust and companionship and compromise and commitment. And about working through things together. Keeping your own identity, certainly. But as partners."

Grace blinks hard and looks away while sadness and futility overwhelm me.

"I don't know how to do it that way," she says, her voice growing distant. "I never have. And I don't know that I'll ever change."

I already know this about Grace. Have always known it, in fact. But I am weary. Tired of the struggle.

"This is nice," she says suddenly, her voice warm. "Talking like this, I mean. I've missed it."

Right now I just want her to stop being nice. It is much easier to let go of Grace the bitch.

Now she is grinning as she reaches out and taps the front of the baseball cap I'd pulled on that morning to cover the mess that sleep had made of my hair overnight. "You're kind of cute in that hat."

I'd forgotten that I was wearing the cap and the T-shirt that I'd slept in and am mortified. I tug at the hat and grimace, my cheeks growing hot. "I just rolled out of bed."

"You look adorable."

I harrumph loudly and look away while I put the coffee mug to my lips. Then I ask the question that has hounded me from the moment I saw that first billboard.

"So tell me," I begin. "Did you just stop loving me? Or did you decide that I'd never fit in to your life?" I pause and search her face. A decade of doubt begins to pile up, and too many of my fears erupt behind my eyes. "Do I embarrass you? Is it that you're ashamed of me?"

Her jaw drops. "God, no, Liz. Whatever gave you that idea? Why would you even ask such a thing?"

I grow embarrassed, and realize that now I am the one who is displaying her vulnerability. My face colors and I drop my gaze as I shrug. "I don't know. Just a guess, really. You've never introduced me to anyone, particularly as your lover. You have a glamorous job. You come from a wealthy family. And I . . . Well, I don't."

Grace is shaking her head and clucking her tongue. "Oh, honey," she sighs. "You are such a sensitive creature." She is smiling, one side of her mouth turning up as she appraises me.

"I've never introduced you to anyone because we're never around anyone I know. We're always traipsing from one city to another."

I'm beginning to feel silly as I realize that this is true. "Okay," I say sheepishly. "You've probably got a good excuse there."

"And as far as the celebrity thing . . ." She pauses, choosing her words carefully. "You have no idea what it's like having to be 'on' all the time. It's actually refreshing that you don't treat me any differently."

She is smiling softly as she continues. "Some people might think that your career is awfully

141

glamorous as well. Leaving the security of your old job and starting all over couldn't have been easy. I'm proud of you for taking that risk. And for how well you're doing."

She laughs. "And, honey, that stuff about us coming from different sides of the tracks was the same shit you harped on twelve years ago when you crushed my very young and very vulnerable heart." She was raising both eyebrows now, her tone changing, becoming lively and teasing.

"I told you that back then?"

"Yes. You dumped me and gave me some line about how I was too good for you and how when I grew up I'd understand." Her voice begins to take on an edge. "It was bullshit then and it's bullshit now. You dumped me for Connie. Period."

I laugh now, enjoying the old game.

"And you dumped me because . . . " I dangle the sentence, mocking her.

"I never dumped you." She lifts her chin haughtily.

"Ha. You have a terrible memory," I tell her.

"Yeah. And yours is a pain in the ass. You remember every detail." She is grinning.

"Exactly my point. Which is why I know that *you* dumped *me*."

"Never, Liz." She shakes her head stubbornly.

"Then what are you doing right now if it's not dumping me? Again." I ask the question without meaning to, and as our eyes meet I feel the pain from three months of frustration and hurt and anger begin to choke me.

Her mouth is a straight line, but her eyes are wounded. "I'm not dumping you," she says quietly.

"No. You'd never call it that, anyway."

"I'm not dumping you, Liz." She repeats herself, her voice tight.

"Then what *are* you doing, Grace? What are you doing here?"

"I don't know. I hated that you left like that." Her voice sounds far away, and I recognize her hedging. She is quite good at hedging.

My humor has vanished and my voice sounds tired. "That's not good enough, Grace. You let me twist in the wind for three months. Without so much as a phone call. You were pissed when I came to New York —"

"I was angry with myself. Not with you," she interrupts.

I wait for her to explain.

"I was insulating myself against everything. When you showed up out of nowhere it woke me up. I saw what I'd done to you, and I knew that I was doing it again." Her eyes were dark. "That I was taking the easy way out."

"So why are you here now?" I ask again.

"I'm not sure." Again her voice drifts quietly, and my frustration grows again.

"You're a coward, Grace."

Her face registers the same shock that I am feeling. I can't believe I've said these words to her. But now that I've opened the door, I decide to step through to the other side.

"Why can't you just be honest with me? What can you possibly say that will hurt me any more than I already do? Why can't you just tell me that it's over and that you don't love me?"

"Because that's not how I feel," she explodes.

"Dammit, Liz. I'm scared. I don't know what to do anymore." She is searching my eyes as I bite my tongue and wait for her to continue. "My feelings haven't changed at all. I love you. I always have. It's the most constant thing I've ever known in my life."

My heart turns over. *She loves me.*

"So why are we going through this?" I ask.

"Because it's not that simple. It's more complicated than loving each other, and you know it."

"You're so practical," I tease her, hope finding a small crack in my heart.

"And you're a romantic. Completely out of touch with reality," she retorts.

I throw back my head and laugh.

"So tell me why it can't possibly work, Grace." I am mocking her, and she knows it.

"I told you. We live on opposite sides of the country. I don't want to give up my job. You hate New York. And even if you didn't, I would never ask you to give up what you have here."

I study her for a moment. "You're right. I hate New York," I grin.

"I'm glad you find this so amusing." Her annoyance is bubbling, and I'm not quite sure why I am feeling so lighthearted. But my tone grows serious.

"Grace." I turn to face her squarely. "Even if I loved New York, you wouldn't ask me to move, would you? Not because you wouldn't want to. But because you'd never open yourself up that way. You'd never let yourself be that vulnerable."

She is staring at me, blinking. "Sometimes I hate it that you know me so well," she says finally.

I chuckle softly. "So tell me what you want, Grace."

144

"I want it all," she says stubbornly. "But I don't believe for one moment that I can have it."

"Well, that's your first mistake. You have to believe."

She rolls her eyes, and I am reminded that she is so pragmatic.

"Don't make me pull teeth, Grace. If I have to ask, then I won't trust the answer."

She takes a deep breath and lets out a sigh. "Nothing has changed, Liz. I don't want to lose you. Ever. I love you. And I want us to be together. I just don't know how to make that happen." Her eyes are wide before her lashes flutter down.

My heart turns to butter as her words wash over me. The hurt and anger of the past few months evaporate as hope begins to swell in my chest. I reach out a hand, and she takes it, turning it over in hers and examining it closely.

"So where do we go from here?" My mind is already fast-forwarding, and I envision us house hunting together. Outside of the city somewhere. Maybe Connecticut. Grace would probably hate the commute, but the hours she worked would help her avoid the traffic. "What do you want to do?" I ask softly, smiling.

"I don't know." Her shoulders lift in a shrug. "I want to keep seeing you."

I can feel the smile tightening on my face.

"Does that mean we should start house hunting in Connecticut?" I venture.

"*Connecticut?*" She is recoiling as she nearly pulls her hands from mine. "God, no." Her laugh is almost a sneer. "I want to keep living in the city. I love my condo."

145

My smile freezes before it falls. She doesn't say *we*. She doesn't ask what I want.

"You've already bought a condo?" I ask.

She nods, suddenly biting her lip.

Hope vaporizes, quickly replaced with a sick, dull ache in my stomach.

"Grace," I begin, my voice not quite steady. "I need you to be very clear with me. What exactly do you want from me?"

Again the shrug as she grows uncomfortable and agitated, hating to be pinned down. "I want to keep seeing you." Her voice is uncharacteristically small.

I hate her evasiveness. "How often?"

"Like before, I guess. I thought you could come and visit once a month or so. We could take vacations together."

I can hear the beating of my heart in my own ears.

"Grace." I am having trouble speaking, and I begin to over-enunciate each word as it forms on my lips. "We were going to live together in San Diego. You told me you wanted to share a home together. You said you wanted a puppy. You said you wanted us to be together." I swallow hard, my mouth suddenly dry. "Now you're telling me that you simply want to date me."

Her eyes are wide now. "Just for a while," she says finally. "Until we see how things work out."

For a moment I almost buy into it. I am so eager that I'm almost content with the offering she is proposing, however meager.

But then reality sinks in as memories crowd my mind. What she really wants from me is next to nothing. An occasional weekend together. No promises. No commitment. No future. No white picket fence or puppy.

I can never trust her. The realization hits me like a slap in the face. I would spend each month agonizing about whether or not there would even be another visit. And each time a few days went by without a word from her, my struggle would begin. I would always wonder if her silence was the beginning of the end. She would always be in control. And I would always be waiting. I would forever love her more than she loved me.

"You chased me all the way out here to tell me that you wanted to *date* me?" It's almost laughable.

"I couldn't let you go like that. I don't want to lose you." Her tone is defensive.

"I think what you *don't* want is a guilty conscience," I say point-blank, without emotion. "And what you *do* want is to keep me around just enough so that you have someone to count on, but not enough to interfere with your life."

She stares at me dumbly. "That's cold, Liz."

I nod slowly. "But true. Isn't it?"

"Of course not," she replies quickly. But she doesn't follow up the words with any others, even as I stare into her eyes and silently beg her to tell me I'm wrong.

Sadness grips me. "It was all a lie." My voice is quiet, barely audible. "It meant nothing to you."

"Liz. That's not true."

"So we would see each other twelve times a year. Plus vacations, of course." I'm growing sarcastic.

The frown on her face grows severe, pulling her eyebrows down together as her lips purse tightly.

"Stop it, Liz. It's not like that. I love you."

My bottom lip is beginning to quiver, and I hate myself for loving her.

"I want to believe that you love me," I tell her, trying to control the crack in my voice. "More than anything in the world." My breath is deep and haggard. "But I don't. And what you're offering just isn't enough. I can't do it."

"So that's it?" Her voice is hollow.

I stare into those brown eyes. The ones that have haunted me for too many long years. Regret fills my heart, and I want nothing more than to take back each word I've just spoken. I want to wrap my arms around her and feel her breath on my cheek. I want to feel the passion explode between us as our mouths find each other. I want to tell her how I love her. How I'd follow her anywhere. That nothing else matters but us.

Slowly, I nod my head as I let her hands slip from mine. "That's it," I say. Then I can't believe I've actually said the words. That I'm finally letting go.

Epilogue

Five years later

I've been standing at the bar just a little longer than I think is necessary. But since it is our friend's brand-new bar, and since it's only been open for one week, I try to remain patient.

I watch the blond bartender serving drinks and flirting with women as she mixes a variety of liquids, and realize she is half my age. I'm beginning to feel old. Scratch that. I've been feeling like I'm getting old for some time now.

Since it looks like I have a long wait ahead of me, I take the opportunity to glance around and take in the decor. The music in the room next door is too loud for my taste, but this room is nice and quiet. The bar itself runs the entire length of one wall. Behind me are scores of tables and booths in intimate settings that allow for easy conversation. Couples huddle together in the dim lights and stare into each other's eyes. Others are laughing, joking around.

A pool table stands in one far corner, several women playing or watching the game. Large television sets line the walls, and my eyes fall to the one directly above and behind the bar. It's early in the evening yet, and the local sportscaster is wrapping up his segment before a slew of commercials begin to play.

"What can I get ya?" The blond bartender is smiling at me. I smile in return and order a couple of beers.

The woman who has been sitting on the bar stool beside me flashes a quick smile before vacating her seat, and I lift one leg and place my foot over the rung possessively.

The national news comes on the air and I watch. Not because I'm particularly interested, but because my choices are to stare at the bartender's bare midriff or to keep my eyes firmly planted on the television. The anchor is unrecognizable to me, and then I remember that it's the weekend and that weekend anchors are the second string. He is talking about some bill that is being held up in congress.

I am vaguely aware that I pay attention to the news anchors and when they're on because of Grace.

It is something she told me about years ago, when describing the different kinds of anchors and what it means to be on at what time.

Two bottles of beer land on the counter before me, and I try not to let my eyes fall to the blond's pierced navel as I smile and toss several bills her way.

I pick up both bottles with one quick glance at the television before I turn away.

"Here with more on the congressional gridlock is Washington correspondent, Grace Sullivan. Grace?"

I nearly drop the beer.

"Thanks, David." Grace's smile is controlled and serious. "*Gridlock* is the perfect word to describe what is currently taking place on Capitol Hill tonight . . ."

My backside finds the stool behind me as I place the beer safely back on the bar. Grace is talking, but either I can't hear or can't understand what she is saying. Her hair is shorter. Soft auburn curls nearly reach her shoulders. I'd forgotten how pretty she is. Her brown eyes are bright, and the curve of her mouth is the same. But she looks older, as if her face is finally beginning to catch up with her age. Which, I calculate quickly, must be nearly forty.

Familiar arms are sliding around my waist. The breath that I've held too long escapes from my lungs and I settle back against my lover's chest.

Grace is smiling now, showing even white teeth. ". . . no one expects this standoff to end any time soon." She pauses. Smiles. "Back to you, David." Her image is gone.

My hands lift, palms sliding along the arms that hold me. "Wow."

My lover gives me a quick squeeze before re-leasing me and sliding onto the stool beside me.

"I guess her dreams came true," I muse.

"At least some of them did." Joanna's voice is quiet, without reproach.

My laugh betrays my feelings. "I was never part of her dreams."

Joanna's eyes are steady. "Maybe. But she was definitely part of yours."

I reach to retrieve the two abandoned bottles of beer and place one in her hands. We haven't talked about Grace in years.

"Yes, she was."

"And now?"

"I don't think about her anymore." I'm reminded of the list I'd made. The list of each and every one of Grace's negative characteristics. The list that I'd taken out and read or added to nearly every day for six months. Then every week or so after that. Until nearly a year had passed.

"She called me last week," I say. "I didn't talk to her. But she left a message."

Joanna's blue eyes barely register surprise.

"I guess now I know why she called. To tell me about her good news."

Joanna searches my face. "Are you going to call her?"

I recognize the hesitancy, the uncertainty in her voice, and my heart turns to putty. I lift one hand and carefully trace the outline of her face, noting the curve of her jaw and the lines that now crease her eyes. Leaning forward, I press my lips to hers and feel her exhale heavily.

When I open my eyes, I take both of her hands in mine and hold them tightly.

"Yes, I'm going to call her."

"I trust you," she says, and I thank her silently.

"You *can* trust me," I tell her.

She nods, accepting my words, and smiles wryly. "I suppose I should thank her, really. If she hadn't shown up five years ago, I don't think we would be together today."

"Possibly," I shrug. "But I don't think so. We would have figured it out eventually."

"Not if you'd moved to New York."

"That was never really an option, remember?"

"Not really. I don't think about any of that stuff anymore. Do you?"

"No." I shake my head, and remember the second list I'd made during that first year after I'd moved out. That list was of everything I valued in a lover. I thought it was the silliest thing my therapist had ever asked me to do. Second to the first list, of course. But I did it anyway, reluctantly.

It took several months before I realized that the woman I was describing on that piece of paper was Joanna.

It took another month or so for me to gather enough courage to show up on the doorstep of our old home. I stepped inside the house, gave the kitties a quick belly rub, then pulled out that sheet of paper and placed it in Joanna's hands.

She read each word silently, then aloud. I looked her square in the eye and told her why I'd made up the list, and that the woman I'd been describing was her.

I'd expected her to send me packing. But she didn't. She just wrapped her arms around me, began to cry, and told me to come back home.

I never left again.

As I stare at my lover now, I've already forgotten Grace.

"Thanks for taking me back," I say, smiling. "Thanks for wanting it to work enough to try again." It hadn't been easy. The beginning was quite painful. We started slowly. Almost dating, really, until the romance was rekindled and the companionship reborn. And trust. We had to build the trust.

Her shrug is nonchalant, playful. "We both just had to get away from each other for a while to realize what we had."

"You mean you didn't know how good you had it until you lost me?" I tease.

"Amy was an awfully good distraction for a little while there," she grins.

I squint back at her. "She was kind of flighty, though."

She laughs. "She was sweet."

"But flighty."

"Okay. Flighty."

We stare at each other, years of love and commitment between us. "I love you, Joanna."

She leans over to kiss me. "I love you, too." When she lifts her head, her eyes are twinkling. "Have I told you happy birthday yet today?"

I groan. "Too many times."

"Was it mean of me to throw this little party for you?"

I'd forgotten about the friends that we'd

abandoned at a table several yards away. "Yes. It was mean," I tell her straight-faced.

She laughs and squeezes my hand.

"Do you know what the best part of turning forty-five is?" I ask.

"*Is* there anything good about turning forty-five?"

"Yes. The best part is knowing that you'll be turning fifty before the year is over."

"Ouch!" She reaches out and tugs my ear playfully. Then she stands and draws me to my feet. "Come on, birthday girl. Time to get back to the party."

She gets a few feet away before I catch up and turn her around to face me. "I've got a better idea. Let's go home." My eyebrows do a little dance, and I watch a slow smile spread across her face.

She tilts her head to one side and eyes me closely before leaning in and planting a kiss on my mouth that I feel all the way to my toes.

Our friends all observe the kiss and are hollering now, whooping it up and clapping loudly. We turn and bow. Then Joanna is blowing them kisses as she links her arm through mine.

"You know what?" She is smiling as she turns to face me. "I'd like nothing more than to go home with you right now. I have a very special present planned for you, you know." She is grinning coyly. Suggestively.

"Oh, really?" I raise one brow and think about the evening ahead. The passion that begins to uncurl inside of me is slow and certain, as sure and steady as the life Joanna and I share.

Years ago I would have grabbed her hand and

headed for the door. But today I can gaze into her eyes and know that there is no need to hurry. There is only the savoring of the moment. Of every moment.

I reach for her hand and give it a quick squeeze. "The anticipation will drive me wild, but I suppose we should stick it out for awhile."

"Driving you wild is exactly what I had in mind," she whispers suggestively.

Her smile is slow and knowing. Full of promise.

A few of the publications of
THE NAIAD PRESS, INC.
P.O. Box 10543   Tallahassee, Florida 32302
Phone (850) 539-5965
Toll-Free Order Number: 1-800-533-1973
Web Site: WWW.NAIADPRESS.COM
Mail orders welcome. Please include 15% postage.
Write or call for our free catalog which also features an
incredible selection of lesbian videos.

FIFTH WHEEL by Kate Calloway. 224 pp. 5th Cassidy James
mystery.   ISBN 1-56280-218-6 $11.95

JUST YESTERDAY by Linda Hill. 176 pp. Reliving all the
passion of yesterday.   ISBN 1-56280-219-4   11.95

THE TOUCH OF YOUR HAND edited by Barbara Grier and
Christine Cassidy. 304 pp. Erotic love stories by Naiad Press
authors.   ISBN 1-56280-220-8   14.95

WINDROW GARDEN by Janet McClellan. 192 pp. They discover
a passion they never dreamed possible.   ISBN 1-56280-216-X   11.95

PAST DUE by Claire McNab. 224 pp. 10th Carol Ashton
mystery.   ISBN 1-56280-217-8   11.95

CHRISTABEL by Laura Adams. 224 pp. Two captive hearts and
the passion that will set them free.   ISBN 1-56280-214-3   11.95

PRIVATE PASSIONS by Laura DeHart Young. 192 pp. An
unforgettable new portrait of lesbian love . . .   ISBN 1-56280-215-1   11.95

BAD MOON RISING by Barbara Johnson. 208 pp. 2nd Colleen
Fitzgerald mystery.   ISBN 1-56280-211-9   11.95

RIVER QUAY by Janet McClellan. 208 pp. 3rd Tru North
mystery.   ISBN 1-56280-212-7   11.95

ENDLESS LOVE by Lisa Shapiro. 272 pp. To believe, once
again, that love can be forever.   ISBN 1-56280-213-5   11.95

FALLEN FROM GRACE by Pat Welch. 256 pp. 6th Helen Black
mystery.   ISBN 1-56280-209-7   11.95

THE NAKED EYE by Catherine Ennis. 208 pp. Her lover in the
camera's eye . . .   ISBN 1-56280-210-0   11.95

OVER THE LINE by Tracey Richardson. 176 pp. 2nd Stevie
Houston mystery.   ISBN 1-56280-202-X   11.95

JULIA'S SONG by Ann O'Leary. 208 pp. Strangely
disturbing . . . strangely exciting.   ISBN 1-56280-197-X   11.95

LOVE IN THE BALANCE by Marianne K. Martin. 256 pp.
Weighing the costs of love . . .   ISBN 1-56280-199-6   11.95

PIECE OF MY HEART by Julia Watts. 208 pp. All the
stuff that dreams are made of —   ISBN 1-56280-206-2   11.95

MAKING UP FOR LOST TIME by Karin Kallmaker. 240 pp.
Nobody does it better . . .   ISBN 1-56280-196-1   11.95

GOLD FEVER by Lyn Denison. 224 pp. By author of *Dream
Lover.*   ISBN 1-56280-201-1   11.95

WHEN THE DEAD SPEAK by Therese Szymanski. 224 pp. 2nd
Brett Higgins mystery.   ISBN 1-56280-198-8   11.95

FOURTH DOWN by Kate Calloway. 240 pp. 4th Cassidy James
mystery.   ISBN 1-56280-205-4   11.95

A MOMENT'S INDISCRETION by Peggy J. Herring. 176 pp.
There's a fine line between love and lust . . .   ISBN 1-56280-194-5   11.95

CITY LIGHTS/COUNTRY CANDLES by Penny Hayes. 208 pp.
About the women she has known . . .   ISBN 1-56280-195-3   11.95

POSSESSIONS by Kaye Davis. 240 pp. 2nd Maris Middleton
mystery.   ISBN 1-56280-192-9   11.95

A QUESTION OF LOVE by Saxon Bennett. 208 pp. Every
woman is granted one great love.   ISBN 1-56280-205-4   11.95

RHYTHM TIDE by Frankie J. Jones. 160 pp.   . . . to desire
passionately and be passionately desired.   ISBN 1-56280-189-9   11.95

PENN VALLEY PHOENIX by Janet McClellan. 208 pp. 2nd
Tru North Mystery.   ISBN 1-56280-200-3   11.95

BY RESERVATION ONLY by Jackie Calhoun. 240 pp. A
chance for true happiness.   ISBN 1-56280-191-0   11.95

OLD BLACK MAGIC by Jaye Maiman. 272 pp. 9th Robin
Miller mystery.   ISBN 1-56280-175-9   11.95

LEGACY OF LOVE by Marianne K. Martin. 240 pp. Women
will do anything for her . . .   ISBN 1-56280-184-8   11.95

LETTING GO by Ann O'Leary. 160 pp. Laura, at 39, in love
with 23-year-old Kate.   ISBN 1-56280-183-X   11.95

LADY BE GOOD edited by Barbara Grier and Christine Cassidy.
288 pp. Erotic stories by Naiad Press authors.   ISBN 1-56280-180-5   14.95

CHAIN LETTER by Claire McNab. 288 pp. 9th Carol Ashton
mystery.   ISBN 1-56280-181-3   11.95

NIGHT VISION by Laura Adams. 256 pp. Erotic fantasy romance
by "famous" author.   ISBN 1-56280-182-1   11.95

SEA TO SHINING SEA by Lisa Shapiro. 256 pp. Unable to resist
the raging passion . . .   ISBN 1-56280-177-5   11.95

THIRD DEGREE by Kate Calloway. 224 pp. 3rd Cassidy James
mystery.   ISBN 1-56280-185-6   11.95

WHEN THE DANCING STOPS by Therese Szymanski. 272 pp.
1st Brett Higgins mystery.   ISBN 1-56280-186-4   11.95

PHASES OF THE MOON by Julia Watts. 192 pp. . . . . hungry
for everything life has to offer.   ISBN 1-56280-176-7   11.95

BABY IT'S COLD by Jaye Maiman. 256 pp. 5th Robin Miller
mystery.   ISBN 1-56280-156-2   10.95

CLASS REUNION by Linda Hill. 176 pp. The girl from her
past . . .   ISBN 1-56280-178-3   11.95

DREAM LOVER by Lyn Denison. 224 pp. A soft, sensuous,
romantic fantasy.   ISBN 1-56280-173-1   11.95

FORTY LOVE by Diana Simmonds. 288 pp. Joyous, heart-
warming romance.   ISBN 1-56280-171-6   11.95

IN THE MOOD by Robbi Sommers. 160 pp. The queen of
erotic tension!   ISBN 1-56280-172-4   11.95

SWIMMING CAT COVE by Lauren Douglas. 192 pp. 2nd
Allison O'Neil Mystery.   ISBN 1-56280-168-6   11.95

THE LOVING LESBIAN by Claire McNab and Sharon Gedan.
240 pp. Explore the experiences that make lesbian love unique.
                                              ISBN 1-56280-169-4   14.95

COURTED by Celia Cohen. 160 pp. Sparkling romantic
encounter.   ISBN 1-56280-166-X   11.95

SEASONS OF THE HEART by Jackie Calhoun. 240 pp. Romance
through the years.   ISBN 1-56280-167-8   11.95

K. C. BOMBER by Janet McClellan. 208 pp. 1st Tru North
mystery.   ISBN 1-56280-157-0   11.95

LAST RITES by Tracey Richardson. 192 pp. 1st Stevie Houston
mystery.   ISBN 1-56280-164-3   11.95

EMBRACE IN MOTION by Karin Kallmaker. 256 pp. A whirlwind
love affair.   ISBN 1-56280-165-1   11.95

HOT CHECK by Peggy J. Herring. 192 pp. Will workaholic Alice
fall for guitarist Ricky?   ISBN 1-56280-163-5   11.95

OLD TIES by Saxon Bennett. 176 pp. Can Cleo surrender to a
passionate new love?   ISBN 1-56280-159-7   11.95

LOVE ON THE LINE by Laura DeHart Young. 176 pp. Will Stef
win Kay's heart?   ISBN 1-56280-162-7   11.95

DEVIL'S LEG CROSSING by Kaye Davis. 192 pp. 1st Maris
Middleton mystery.   ISBN 1-56280-158-9   11.95

COSTA BRAVA by Marta Balletbo Coll. 144 pp. Read the book,
see the movie!   ISBN 1-56280-153-8   11.95

MEETING MAGDALENE & OTHER STORIES by
Marilyn Freeman. 144 pp. Read the book, see the movie!
                                              ISBN 1-56280-170-8   11.95

SECOND FIDDLE by Kate 208 pp. 2nd P.I. Cassidy James
mystery.   ISBN 1-56280-169-6   11.95

LAUREL by Isabel Miller. 128 pp. By the author of the beloved
Patience and Sarah.   ISBN 1-56280-146-5   10.95

LOVE OR MONEY by Jackie Calhoun. 240 pp. The romance of
real life.   ISBN 1-56280-147-3   10.95

SMOKE AND MIRRORS by Pat Welch. 224 pp. 5th Helen Black
Mystery.   ISBN 1-56280-143-0   10.95

DANCING IN THE DARK edited by Barbara Grier & Christine
Cassidy. 272 pp. Erotic love stories by Naiad Press authors.
                                            ISBN 1-56280-144-9   14.95

TIME AND TIME AGAIN by Catherine Ennis. 176 pp. Passionate
love affair.   ISBN 1-56280-145-7   10.95

PAXTON COURT by Diane Salvatore. 256 pp. Erotic and wickedly
funny contemporary tale about the business of learning to live
together.   ISBN 1-56280-114-7   10.95

INNER CIRCLE by Claire McNab. 208 pp. 8th Carol Ashton
Mystery.   ISBN 1-56280-135-X   11.95

LESBIAN SEX: AN ORAL HISTORY by Susan Johnson.
240 pp. Need we say more?   ISBN 1-56280-142-2   14.95

WILD THINGS by Karin Kallmaker. 240 pp. By the undisputed
mistress of lesbian romance.   ISBN 1-56280-139-2   11.95

THE GIRL NEXT DOOR by Mindy Kaplan. 208 pp. Just what
you d expect.   ISBN 1-56280-140-6   11.95

NOW AND THEN by Penny Hayes. 240 pp. Romance on the
westward journey.   ISBN 1-56280-121-X   11.95

HEART ON FIRE by Diana Simmonds. 176 pp. The romantic and
erotic rival of *Curious Wine*.   ISBN 1-56280-152-X   11.95

DEATH AT LAVENDER BAY by Lauren Wright Douglas. 208 pp.
1st Allison O'Neil Mystery.   ISBN 1-56280-085-X   11.95

YES I SAID YES I WILL by Judith McDaniel. 272 pp. Hot
romance by famous author.   ISBN 1-56280-138-4   11.95

FORBIDDEN FIRES by Margaret C. Anderson. Edited by Mathilda
Hills. 176 pp. Famous author's "unpublished" Lesbian romance.
                                            ISBN 1-56280-123-6   21.95

SIDE TRACKS by Teresa Stores. 160 pp. Gender-bending
Lesbians on the road.   ISBN 1-56280-122-8   10.95

HOODED MURDER by Annette Van Dyke. 176 pp. 1st Jessie
Batelle Mystery.   ISBN 1-56280-134-1   10.95

WILDWOOD FLOWERS by Julia Watts. 208 pp. Hilarious and
heart-warming tale of true love.   ISBN 1-56280-127-9   10.95

NEVER SAY NEVER by Linda Hill. 224 pp. Rule #1: Never get involved with . . . ISBN 1-56280-126-0   11.95

THE SEARCH by Melanie McAllester. 240 pp. Exciting top cop Tenny Mendoza case. ISBN 1-56280-150-3   10.95

THE WISH LIST by Saxon Bennett. 192 pp. Romance through the years. ISBN 1-56280-125-2   10.95

FIRST IMPRESSIONS by Kate 208 pp. 1st P.I. Cassidy James mystery. ISBN 1-56280-133-3   10.95

OUT OF THE NIGHT by Kris Bruyer. 192 pp. Spine-tingling thriller. ISBN 1-56280-120-1   10.95

NORTHERN BLUE by Tracey Richardson. 224 pp. Police recruits Miki & Miranda — passion in the line of fire. ISBN 1-56280-118-X   10.95

LOVE'S HARVEST by Peggy J. Herring. 176 pp. by the author of *Once More With Feeling*. ISBN 1-56280-117-1   10.95

THE COLOR OF WINTER by Lisa Shapiro. 208 pp. Romantic love beyond your wildest dreams. ISBN 1-56280-116-3   10.95

FAMILY SECRETS by Laura DeHart Young. 208 pp. Enthralling romance and suspense. ISBN 1-56280-119-8   10.95

INLAND PASSAGE by Jane Rule. 288 pp. Tales exploring conventional & unconventional relationships. ISBN 0-930044-56-8   10.95

DOUBLE BLUFF by Claire McNab. 208 pp. 7th Carol Ashton Mystery. ISBN 1-56280-096-5   10.95

BAR GIRLS by Lauran Hoffman. 176 pp. See the movie, read the book! ISBN 1-56280-115-5   10.95

THE FIRST TIME EVER edited by Barbara Grier & Christine Cassidy. 272 pp. Love stories by Naiad Press authors. ISBN 1-56280-086-8   14.95

MISS PETTIBONE AND MISS McGRAW by Brenda Weathers. 208 pp. A charming ghostly love story. ISBN 1-56280-151-1   10.95

CHANGES by Jackie Calhoun. 208 pp. Involved romance and relationships. ISBN 1-56280-083-3   10.95

FAIR PLAY by Rose Beecham. 256 pp. An Amanda Valentine Mystery. ISBN 1-56280-081-7   10.95

PAYBACK by Celia Cohen. 176 pp. A gripping thriller of romance, revenge and betrayal. ISBN 1-56280-084-1   10.95

THE BEACH AFFAIR by Barbara Johnson. 224 pp. Sizzling summer romance/mystery/intrigue. ISBN 1-56280-090-6   10.95

GETTING THERE by Robbi Sommers. 192 pp. Nobody does it like Robbi! ISBN 1-56280-099-X   10.95

FINAL CUT by Lisa Haddock. 208 pp. 2nd Carmen Ramirez Mystery. ISBN 1-56280-088-4   10.95

FLASHPOINT by Katherine V. Forrest. 256 pp. A Lesbian
blockbuster!   ISBN 1-56280-079-5   10.95

CLAIRE OF THE MOON by Nicole Conn. Audio Book —
Read by Marianne Hyatt.   ISBN 1-56280-113-9   16.95

FOR LOVE AND FOR LIFE: INTIMATE PORTRAITS OF
LESBIAN COUPLES by Susan Johnson. 224 pp.
                                  ISBN 1-56280-091-4   14.95

DEVOTION by Mindy Kaplan. 192 pp. See the movie — read
the book!   ISBN 1-56280-093-0   10.95

SOMEONE TO WATCH by Jaye Maiman. 272 pp. 4th Robin
Miller Mystery.   ISBN 1-56280-095-7   10.95

GREENER THAN GRASS by Jennifer Fulton. 208 pp. A young
woman — a stranger in her bed.   ISBN 1-56280-092-2   10.95

TRAVELS WITH DIANA HUNTER by Regine Sands. Erotic
lesbian romp. Audio Book (2 cassettes)   ISBN 1-56280-107-4   16.95

CABIN FEVER by Carol Schmidt. 256 pp. Sizzling suspense
and passion.   ISBN 1-56280-089-1   10.95

THERE WILL BE NO GOODBYES by Laura DeHart Young. 192
pp. Romantic love, strength, and friendship.   ISBN 1-56280-103-1   10.95

FAULTLINE by Sheila Ortiz Taylor. 144 pp. Joyous comic
lesbian novel.   ISBN 1-56280-108-2   9.95

OPEN HOUSE by Pat Welch. 176 pp. 4th Helen Black Mystery.
                                    ISBN 1-56280-102-3   10.95

ONCE MORE WITH FEELING by Peggy J. Herring. 240 pp.
Lighthearted, loving romantic adventure.   ISBN 1-56280-089-2   11.95

FOREVER by Evelyn Kennedy. 224 pp. Passionate romance — love
overcoming all obstacles.   ISBN 1-56280-094-9   10.95

WHISPERS by Kris Bruyer. 176 pp. Romantic ghost story.
                                  ISBN 1-56280-082-5   10.95

NIGHT SONGS by Penny Mickelbury. 224 pp. 2nd Gianna
Maglione Mystery.   ISBN 1-56280-097-3   10.95

GETTING TO THE POINT by Teresa Stores. 256 pp. Classic
southern Lesbian novel.   ISBN 1-56280-100-7   10.95

PAINTED MOON by Karin Kallmaker. 224 pp. Delicious
Kallmaker romance.   ISBN 1-56280-075-2   11.95

THE MYSTERIOUS NAIAD edited by Katherine V. Forrest &
Barbara Grier. 320 pp. Love stories by Naiad Press authors.
                                  ISBN 1-56280-074-4   14.95

DAUGHTERS OF A CORAL DAWN by Katherine V. Forrest.
240 pp. Tenth Anniversary Edition.   ISBN 1-56280-104-X   11.95

BODY GUARD by Claire McNab. 208 pp. 6th Carol Ashton
Mystery.   ISBN 1-56280-073-6   11.95

CACTUS LOVE by Lee Lynch. 192 pp. Stories by the beloved
storyteller.   ISBN 1-56280-071-X   9.95

SECOND GUESS by Rose Beecham. 216 pp. An Amanda
Valentine Mystery.   ISBN 1-56280-069-8   9.95

A RAGE OF MAIDENS by Lauren Wright Douglas. 240 pp.
6th Caitlin Reece Mystery.   ISBN 1-56280-068-X   10.95

TRIPLE EXPOSURE by Jackie Calhoun. 224 pp. Romantic
drama involving many characters.   ISBN 1-56280-067-1   10.95

PERSONAL ADS by Robbi Sommers. 176 pp. Sizzling short
stories.   ISBN 1-56280-059-0   11.95

CROSSWORDS by Penny Sumner. 256 pp. 2nd Victoria Cross
Mystery.   ISBN 1-56280-064-7   9.95

SWEET CHERRY WINE by Carol Schmidt. 224 pp. A novel of
suspense.   ISBN 1-56280-063-9   9.95

CERTAIN SMILES by Dorothy Tell. 160 pp. Erotic short stories.
                                                ISBN 1-56280-066-3   9.95

EDITED OUT by Lisa Haddock. 224 pp. 1st Carmen Ramirez
Mystery.   ISBN 1-56280-077-9   9.95

WEDNESDAY NIGHTS by Camarin Grae. 288 pp. Sexy
adventure.   ISBN 1-56280-060-4   11.95

SMOKEY O by Celia Cohen. 176 pp. Relationships on the
playing field.   ISBN 1-56280-057-4   9.95

KATHLEEN O'DONALD by Penny Hayes. 256 pp. Rose and
Kathleen find each other and employment in 1909 NYC.
                                                ISBN 1-56280-070-1   9.95

STAYING HOME by Elisabeth Nonas. 256 pp. Molly and Alix
want a baby . . . or do they?   ISBN 1-56280-076-0   10.95

TRUE LOVE by Jennifer Fulton. 240 pp. Six lesbians searching
for love in all the "right" places.   ISBN 1-56280-035-3   11.95

KEEPING SECRETS by Penny Mickelbury. 208 pp. 1st Gianna
Maglione Mystery.   ISBN 1-56280-052-3   9.95

THE ROMANTIC NAIAD edited by Katherine V. Forrest &
Barbara Grier. 336 pp. Love stories by Naiad Press authors.
                                                ISBN 1-56280-054-X   14.95

UNDER MY SKIN by Jaye Maiman. 336 pp. 3rd Robin Miller
Mystery.   ISBN 1-56280-049-3.   11.95

CAR POOL by Karin Kallmaker. 272pp. Lesbians on wheels
and then some!   ISBN 1-56280-048-5   11.95

NOT TELLING MOTHER: STORIES FROM A LIFE by Diane
Salvatore. 176 pp. Her 3rd novel.   ISBN 1-56280-044-2   9.95

GOBLIN MARKET by Lauren Wright Douglas. 240pp. 5th Caitlin
Reece Mystery.   ISBN 1-56280-047-7   10.95

FRIENDS AND LOVERS by Jackie Calhoun. 224 pp. Midwestern Lesbian lives and loves. ISBN 1-56280-041-8   11.95

BEHIND CLOSED DOORS by Robbi Sommers. 192 pp. Hot, erotic short stories. ISBN 1-56280-039-6   11.95

CLAIRE OF THE MOON by Nicole Conn. 192 pp. See the movie — read the book! ISBN 1-56280-038-8   11.95

SILENT HEART by Claire McNab. 192 pp. Exotic Lesbian romance. ISBN 1-56280-036-1   11.95

THE SPY IN QUESTION by Amanda Kyle Williams. 256 pp. A Madison McGuire Mystery. ISBN 1-56280-037-X   9.95

SAVING GRACE by Jennifer Fulton. 240 pp. Adventure and romantic entanglement. ISBN 1-56280-051-5   11.95

CURIOUS WINE by Katherine V. Forrest. 176 pp. Tenth Anniversary Edition. The most popular contemporary Lesbian love story.
ISBN 1-56280-053-1   11.95
     Audio Book (2 cassettes)   ISBN 1-56280-105-8   16.95

CHAUTAUQUA by Catherine Ennis. 192 pp. Exciting, romantic adventure. ISBN 1-56280-032-9   9.95

A PROPER BURIAL by Pat Welch. 192 pp. 3rd Helen Black Mystery. ISBN 1-56280-033-7   9.95

SILVERLAKE HEAT: A Novel of Suspense by Carol Schmidt. 240 pp. Rhonda is as hot as Laney's dreams. ISBN 1-56280-031-0   9.95

LOVE, ZENA BETH by Diane Salvatore. 224 pp. The most talked about lesbian novel of the nineties! ISBN 1-56280-030-2   10.95

A DOORYARD FULL OF FLOWERS by Isabel Miller. 160 pp. Stories incl. 2 sequels to *Patience and Sarah.* ISBN 1-56280-029-9   9.95

MURDER BY TRADITION by Katherine V. Forrest. 288 pp. 4th Kate Delafield Mystery. ISBN 1-56280-002-7   11.95

THE EROTIC NAIAD edited by Katherine V. Forrest & Barbara Grier. 224 pp. Love stories by Naiad Press authors.
ISBN 1-56280-026-4   14.95

DEAD CERTAIN by Claire McNab. 224 pp. 5th Carol Ashton Mystery. ISBN 1-56280-027-2   9.95

CRAZY FOR LOVING by Jaye Maiman. 320 pp. 2nd Robin Miller Mystery. ISBN 1-56280-025-6   11.95

UNCERTAIN COMPANIONS by Robbi Sommers. 204 pp. Steamy, erotic novel. ISBN 1-56280-017-5   11.95

A TIGER'S HEART by Lauren W. Douglas. 240 pp. 4th Caitlin Reece Mystery. ISBN 1-56280-018-3   9.95

PAPERBACK ROMANCE by Karin Kallmaker. 256 pp. A delicious romance. ISBN 1-56280-019-1   10.95

THE LAVENDER HOUSE MURDER by Nikki Baker. 224 pp.
2nd Virginia Kelly Mystery. ISBN 1-56280-012-4   9.95

PASSION BAY by Jennifer Fulton. 224 pp. Passionate romance,
virgin beaches, tropical skies. ISBN 1-56280-028-0   10.95

STICKS AND STONES by Jackie Calhoun. 208 pp. Contemporary
lesbian lives and loves. ISBN 1-56280-020-5   9.95
Audio Book (2 cassettes) ISBN 1-56280-106-6   16.95

UNDER THE SOUTHERN CROSS by Claire McNab. 192 pp.
Romantic nights Down Under. ISBN 1-56280-011-6   11.95

GRASSY FLATS by Penny Hayes. 256 pp. Lesbian romance in
the '30s. ISBN 1-56280-010-8   9.95

THE END OF APRIL by Penny Sumner. 240 pp. 1st Victoria
Cross Mystery. ISBN 1-56280-007-8   8.95

KISS AND TELL by Robbi Sommers. 192 pp. Scorching stories
by the author of *Pleasures*. ISBN 1-56280-005-1   11.95

STILL WATERS by Pat Welch. 208 pp. 2nd Helen Black Mystery.
ISBN 0-941483-97-5   9.95

TO LOVE AGAIN by Evelyn Kennedy. 208 pp. Wildly romantic
love story. ISBN 0-941483-85-1   11.95

IN THE GAME by Nikki Baker. 192 pp. 1st Virginia Kelly
Mystery. ISBN 1-56280-004-3   9.95

STRANDED by Camarin Grae. 320 pp. Entertaining, riveting
adventure. ISBN 0-941483-99-1   9.95

THE DAUGHTERS OF ARTEMIS by Lauren Wright Douglas.
240 pp. 3rd Caitlin Reece Mystery. ISBN 0-941483-95-9   9.95

CLEARWATER by Catherine Ennis. 176 pp. Romantic secrets
of a small Louisiana town. ISBN 0-941483-65-7   8.95

THE HALLELUJAH MURDERS by Dorothy Tell. 176 pp. 2nd
Poppy Dillworth Mystery. ISBN 0-941483-88-6   8.95

SECOND CHANCE by Jackie Calhoun. 256 pp. Contemporary
Lesbian lives and loves. ISBN 0-941483-93-2   9.95

BENEDICTION by Diane Salvatore. 272 pp. Striking, contemporary romantic novel. ISBN 0-941483-90-8   11.95

TOUCHWOOD by Karin Kallmaker. 240 pp. Loving, May/
December romance. ISBN 0-941483-76-2   11.95

These are just a few of the many Naiad Press titles — we are the oldest and
largest lesbian/feminist publishing company in the world. We also offer an
enormous selection of lesbian video products. Please request a complete
catalog. We offer personal service; we encourage and welcome direct mail
orders from individuals who have limited access to bookstores carrying our
publications.

LOOKING FOR NAIAD?

Buy our books at
www.naiadpress.com

or call our toll-free number
1-800-533-1973

or by fax (24 hours a day)
1-850-539-9731